C. M. Bryden

An Arranged Marriage

Limited Special Edition. No. 10 of 10 Hardbacks

C. M. Bryden is a lady that believes "love conquers all", writing romances fills her retirement days. People-watching often leads to intriguing stories as her imagination makes up scenarios. Once a character has taken root in her imagination, the story leaps ahead.

This book is dedicated to my man in a million, my wonderful husband of many years.

C. M. Bryden

An Arranged Marriage

Austin Macauley Publishers™

LONDON • CAMBRIDGE • NEW YORK • SHARJAH

A CIP catalogue record for this title is available from the British Library.

ISBN 9781788485753 (Paperback)
ISBN 9781788485760 (Hardback)
ISBN 9781528954556 (ePub e-book)

www.austinmacauley.com

First Published (2019)
Austin Macauley Publishers Ltd
25 Canada Square
Canary Wharf
London
E14 5LQ

For my friends who encourage me to follow my dreams.

Table of Contents

Prologue

Jane Reynolds drove into the car park: parking her ancient Mini neatly between her father's old, and much loved Jaguar, and a gleaming black Porsche she eyed enviously, wondering whether its owner was equally as racy!

She strode into the reception area, her high heels tapping on the tiled floor; the only sound to be heard in the deserted building, as she made her way down the corridor towards her father's office.

Pausing for a moment at his door, she ran one hand through her hair, at the same time smoothing imaginary creases from the skirt of her business suit well aware this was an important day in her father's life, at the same time unaware it might possibly be of some importance to hers as well!

Nervously, she composed herself before knocking on the door and waiting for her father's command to enter. There was no response. She knocked again and then, believing the room to be empty, she opened the door and walked in. To her surprise, her father and a much younger man were standing with their heads close together, poring intently over some papers strewn across the desk: it was only the soft thud of the door closing behind her that alerted them to her presence. In unison they turned, watching as she walked towards them. One with pride in his eyes, the other with lust!

Jake Adams had felt his heart lurch in his chest the instant he set eyes on her. He instinctively knew as he watched her walk across the room that he wanted her. He lusted after her and for more than a one-night stand!

Jane smiled at her father, taking in his familiar features, that only months ago had been unlined and boyish, but now were careworn and haggard. His hair, once dark had changed almost overnight to silver.

He smiled at her, more a grimace than a smile. From his expression she could see he was feeling apprehensive, as to the outcome of the proposed meeting with the young man standing at his side. He put his arm around her waist before turning to the young man.

'Jake, I would like you to meet my daughter, Jane.'

The young man stepped forward, taking Jane's hand in his.

'I'm pleased to meet you...' he said, momentarily taken aback by his physical reaction as he looked at her and took hold of her outstretched hand, holding it for just a little longer than was really necessary. His heart and head overwhelmed for a moment or two; stunned as he was by the exquisiteness of her features.

He studied her face and noted her eyes looking at him with interest. Two beautiful shimmering emerald jewels glittered and blazed at him, the likes of which he'd never seen before.

Jake moved his gaze to study her lips, liking what he saw. They were shapely and full, luscious and eminently kissable. So great was his desire to taste them he found it hard not to reach out and pull her into his arms.

By this time his loins were aching with his desire to possess her. As for Jane, she'd found his gaze equally as disturbing. For a few moments the predatory glint in his eyes had startled her to such a degree her already fragile composure was threatening to crumble.

Jake continued to stare at her, until his gaze eventually wandered and she could see him mentally undressing her, his eyes stripping her naked; his desire to devour her apparent.

Suddenly, Jane felt a rush of heat spreading through her body, leaving her cheeks inflamed by his blatant sexual glances, as his eyes sent out messages of his desire, making her emotions run riot.

Jane had never met such a man before, yet her mind and body had instinctively recognised him, assessing him as a possible mate, a primeval reaction towards the man it had surely been her destiny to meet.

Perhaps they'd known each other from a previous existence? It must have been, as Jane knew she'd never met this man before, she would certainly have remembered him! In no more time than it took for her to give him a quick glance nature had taken over her reasoning. It was as if a mist had suddenly been lifted from her eyes and thoughts. At the same time, she could see him quite clearly for what he was, a predator and a hunter, yet she knew he was the man she wanted as the father of her children. He was everything she wanted in a mate. Unaware, for a moment or two, she was subconsciously taking stock of him, she shuddered, returning to the present, knowing deep in her heart that meeting Jake Adams had been a life defining moment for her, a moment in time she would remember forever.

He looked to be in his early thirties, just the right age for her. As far as she was concerned he was the ultimate in tall, dark and handsome! He was extremely good-looking yet apparently unaware of his looks. From what she could see of his well-proportioned physique, he certainly appeared to be no stranger to a regime at the gym!

He wore his dark brown hair unfashionably long, the natural curls and waves that she wanted to run her fingers through, just brushing the collar of his jacket. He stood at least six feet tall, head and shoulders above her, which she particularly liked.

Suddenly she had an urge, she found hard to resist, to reach out and hold him close, to caress him. She wanted, nay needed, his body against hers, to feel for herself the power of his muscles against her, at the same time she wanted more, much more! She drew in her breath taken aback by her carnal thoughts, her body aching with her desire to be possessed.

It must have been the pheromones, exuding from every pore of his body that were affecting her senses, attracting her, enhancing the longing she felt for him, something she'd never experienced before. Her gaze never wavered as she continued to feast her eyes on him, so transfixed was she by his total maleness she suddenly felt faint. Jake Adams was certainly an impressive specimen of manhood, the likes of which Jane Reynolds had never met before.

Meanwhile, as the minutes ticked away, Andrew, standing at his desk watched, transfixed at Jake's reaction to meeting his daughter for the first time. Andrew knew she was intelligent, as well as beautiful, a fine catch for any young man. He could now see for himself how Jake had been unable to tear his eyes away from her. It was a compulsion the young man couldn't resist. A look Andrew couldn't ignore either, unable able to believe the sexual chemistry he'd witnessed between the young couple, something he'd never seen before, and then he realised if Jane and Jake had indeed fallen in love at first sight, it could only bode well for him, and the future of his company!

Jake was still looking at Jane, as one would look at a goddess: her physical beauty filling his eyes and making it imperative that he commit everything about her to his memory: from the colour of her hair, with its lustrous waves of burnished mahogany resting on her shoulders, noting with a smile the way one stray tress had fallen seductively across her eyes.

His eyes had then moved downwards: taking in her womanly curves and the pert breasts he longed to caress; down to the narrowness of her waist, emphasised even further by the cut of her jacket, then on to her womanly hips he wanted to caress as he pulled her close.

He drew in his breath as he imagined how they would feel when he pulled her into his arms and held her, suddenly aware of his arousal, as his body responded quite naturally, to the thoughts of what he intended doing, sooner, rather than later, to the goddess that stood before him.

Jake's eyes continued to travel slowly downwards, until they reached her shapely legs, noticing the ridiculously sexy shoes she wore as she'd walked into the room. One thing was absolutely certain; Jane Reynolds was exactly the kind of woman he liked; sassy, sexy, and much more.

She wasn't like any other woman he'd ever met. He could see she was special, and he also knew he wanted her permanently in his life, instinctively knowing at last he'd met the one woman he'd waited for all his life. To his surprise he wanted to marry her; even more than that, he wanted her to be the mother of his children, an event he'd never thought of before, or even wanted!

Jane was the first to look away, but only after letting her eyes have the final luxury of roaming sensually over him, mirroring his smile, showing her own set of perfect teeth.

She'd taken in the superb cut of the Armani business suit he was wearing, cut to emphasise the broadness of his shoulders and then, the pure whiteness of the silk shirt that accentuated his tan; the top two buttons undone, allowing his dark chest hairs to be just visible, leaving Jane imagining how it would feel as she threaded her fingers through them as she nuzzled close into his chest, as she explored his body for real. The casual elegance of his clothes added to his magnetism and she smiled, a secret smile, her stomach contracting with a longing inside her that was primitive in its origin, exactly as Jake's reaction had been to her. She imagined herself enfolded in his arms, both of them naked, just as nature intended, with nothing coming between them to stifle their desires. She sighed. Her eyes suddenly caught by a gold Rolex, peeping out from under the cuffs of his shirtsleeves. She nearly laughed out loud, it was the finishing touch to the image she had of him as being the perfect man about town.

She looked across at his hands, strong and capable, his fingers long and elegant, and ringless like hers, leaving her to wonder whether he was married, or not? Then, finally, as enamoured as she was by his physical beauty, the mist of love cleared momentarily from her eyes, letting her see another side to him.

She knew exactly the sort of man Jake Adams was. He was arrogant, egotistical and confidently sure of himself, but more than that, he *appeared to be an animal,* a creature so wild that no amount of designer clothing could ever disguise him for something other than what he was.

She could see at heart he really was a panther locked in a man's body as he stood surveying her; his lithe body was poised and ready to pounce. His amber eyes focused on her, waiting for the moment he would capture her as his prey and devour her.

Suddenly, her legs seemed to turn to jelly and she shivered, then paled; a *frisson* of fear and excitement pulsating through her body as she nervously watched him; licking her lips, unconsciously signalling her own sexual interest in him. At the same time, for a moment or two, she was powerless to even move until finally, she found the strength and an inner courage to step forward, where she held onto her father's desk, thankful for the feel of its solid wood beneath her fingers.

For the first time in her life, Jane felt afraid of her future, very afraid, as though a sixth sense was warning her to beware of the man who stood before her; a man whose animal eyes had never left her from the minute she'd walked into the room. This was the man her father was prepared to place his faith in;

believing him to be the saviour of his failing company, but was a failing company *all* that Jake Adams wanted?

Jake, was afraid. Afraid this lovely creature might already be spoken. He wanted her: without a second thought he made a decision he knew would change his life forever.

Had Jane known what was on Jake's mind she would have gone running from the room as though all the devils in hell were after her? But she didn't know, and therein lies what is about to follow.

The room was silent and full of tension, for a few moments no one spoke. Jake looked from Jane to her father and then down at the papers spread out on the desk in front of him. He started to gather them together. Andrew Reynolds watched, open mouthed in astonishment, still unable to believe what he'd witnessed happening between his daughter and this young man, and what he was seeing now as the man he'd thought was going to be his company's saviour was preparing to leave and without any discussion. Andrew was at a loss to know what to do or say!

Jake, suddenly aware his actions were unexpected, looked up and smiled briefly at Andrew, before continuing to place the papers into his briefcase.

'I'll contact you.' He said quietly, 'just as soon as I've studied the accounts and I've come to a decision.'

Andrew nodded in return, fully aware his future and that of his business rested entirely in the hands of the young man who stood before him.

Once he'd finished Jake clicked his briefcase shut. After a brief handshake with Andrew, and a curt nod to Jane, along with a look that left her senses confused and reeling, he left the room, leaving father and daughter to ponder individually on just *what* exactly had taken place.

Little did any of them know much how their lives were about to change with the decision Jake had already made!

As for the fates, they were already laughing at the mischief they'd caused? So, what was the outcome going to be? As it is written! So what will be will be? For Jake and Jane, it was a truism. If something is our destiny, then so be it!

Chapter One

The meeting in Andrew's Reynolds office was the culmination of events that had started two years earlier when his wife, Isabel, had suddenly passed away in her early forties. Her death from a heart attack was as untimely as it was unexpected, and a terrible blow to her husband and to Jane, her only daughter.

After the funeral, Jane had stayed with her father for several weeks at the family home in the country. It was only after watching her moping around the house for several days that Andrew finally insisted it was about time for her to return to her own home and career. He even managed to convince her he would be able to cope on his own and, believing him, Jane returned to London.

At first he seemed to be doing fine with no indication he wasn't coping. She spoke to him often and could detect no sign in his manner or speech that he wasn't.

In the past her father had never discussed the family business with her. Therefore, she had no reason to believe it was anything other than successful as it had been for years, leaving her to assume all was well.

Once back in London the days and weeks soon turned into months, passing quickly for Jane, as they do for those with busy working lives. It wasn't until several months had passed that she began to notice how his tone of voice had changed; first of all, in a subtle way, which didn't at first cause her any alarm. Her suspicions that something might possibly be wrong began only when he suddenly started to sound morose, evading her questions as to how he was feeling and passing off her concerns by telling her he was just tired. Her concerns as to how the business was faring in the current state of the economy he tended to ignore completely, changing the subject by asking about her own business life, until she began to think he might just be suffering with depression; presuming this would be quite normal for someone who'd only recently lost the love of his life. But her father was clever when she voiced her concerns. She'd advised him to see his doctor, but he'd merely fobbed her off, telling her he was fine and not to worry. This appeased her at the time, being busy as well to worry too much about him.

As a senior consultant for a large travel company she was responsible mostly for corporate work. It was part of her job description to frequently travel abroad, where she ran training courses for the company. It was only after she'd returned from one such prolonged trip to Europe, doing just that she realised she hadn't seen her father for some weeks. Of course they'd kept in touch by phone, but Jane knew she needed to visit him, to satisfy her own mind all really was well.

She'd just finished checking her diary, deciding to go the next day and spend a few days with him when Jessie, her assistant and best friend, poked her head round the office door, interrupting her thoughts.

'Are you busy tonight?' she'd asked. 'If not, I've got an outing arranged for us to have our fortunes told!'

Usually sceptical of such things, Jane had laughed, but agreed to go, convincing herself it was for Jessie's benefit, rather than her own, as her friend was recovering from a broken romance and needed cheering up.

'I need to phone my father first. It's about time I went to see him. He probably thinks I've deserted him.'

And so it was, that later that evening, the two young women travelled across the city to learn what the future held in store for them both.

It was Jessie who had the first sitting. Shuffling the tarot cards as instructed, she then placed them in position on the small table in front of her.

Her reading began with the cards showing a failed past relationship. But to her surprise, a new one was in the offing, a relationship the reader interpreted as possibly leading to marriage. At this revelation, Jessie looked quite shocked and amazed. The cards then spelt out something else; that this new relationship might lead her to becoming a mother! That was more than she could bear, it couldn't possibly be true! It was at that point her previous faith in the tarot cards plummeted. She couldn't believe what she'd heard and from a stranger at that, one who knew nothing of her, or her past, or of what had happened a few months ago.

After living with a man she'd loved deeply for fifteen years, but one who'd been afraid of making a commitment to marry her and have children, her partner had suddenly confessed he'd fallen in love with another much younger woman and was going to leave her and marry his much younger new love!

Jessie thought at the time he would soon tire of being with a much younger woman but she'd been wrong; and then shocked, when, within a few weeks he did indeed get married, leaving her broken hearted and sceptical about the male species in general.

Sitting with the tarot cards spread out in front of her, predicting a new and lasting relationship and one, which might possibly lead to marriage was more than Jessie could really believe. And neither did the pronouncement exactly thrill her: her trust in men well was truly dented, especially since she'd loved being part of, as she thought, a loving partnership. She'd loved being a homemaker and had longed for marriage and children, but it wasn't to be. She'd been devastated by her loss and now, as she sat in this stranger's front room, with its well-worn furniture and outdated and old fashioned knickknacks, she suddenly began to feel more optimistic; perhaps the card's predictions would come true and she would meet a wonderful man, trying to convince herself that maybe one day, she *would* become a wife and mother?

There was just one big problem, she was nearly thirty-eight years old and her childbearing years were coming to an end. If it didn't happen soon she would die a childless old maid, something she didn't want to happen!

The evening proved to be a great success, at least in part for Jessie, with the predictions from her cards making her happy. At last it seemed as though her dark clouds really did have silver linings. She couldn't wait to find out what the cards foretold for Jane!

Jane had sat impassively throughout Jessie's session, deep in her own thoughts, until it came to her turn.

Her cards showed two men in her life, with one in particular that would have a profound effect on her future happiness. She'd sat up straight as the reader suddenly caught her interest, well and truly captured, as the tarot cards went on to predict her making a life changing decision.

She'd laughed out loud. It was too preposterous for words to believe that two men and a life changing decision would be her destiny! She didn't think so! Not for one minute! She didn't even have a steady boyfriend, let alone one she liked well enough to want to marry. She'd had a couple of relationships in the past, but both had fizzled out, mainly because she'd put her career first. She hadn't been ready at the time to settle down to being a housewife. As far as she was concerned, she was already married, to her career! The tarot cards might predict marriage but it certainly wasn't on her agenda but then, how many of us really do believe what's been foretold until afterwards, when we look back with hindsight?

Much to Jane's amusement, Jessie was really upbeat at her predictions when they discussed their evening whilst travelling home, absolutely certain her "Mister Right" might possibly be waiting around the next corner, and all she had to do was to make sure she didn't close the door on any eligible young men!

As for Jane, she promptly dismissed her predictions as nonsense, not convinced that a pack of cards could foretell the future for anyone, let alone her! Yet, there'd been something about the card's predictions that brought to mind a troublesome dream she'd been having for some weeks.

It was always the same dream and usually took place in olden times, when pirates and vagabonds sailed the seven seas in galleons. She would dream of being captured and then held prisoner for a ransom. Kept in a dark and spooky old house she couldn't identify, but knew to be by the sea, as she could hear it pounding against what she thought to be rocks. No doubt it really was the sound of her blood rushing through her veins that had triggered her bizarre thoughts.

Her dreams always ended with her being tied up and unable to release herself from her bindings.

Night after night her dream had the same outcome; a dark haired man, dressed as a pirate and brandishing a cutlass, would burst into the room and cut her free, before sweeping her up into his arms, then carrying her off into a misty future, kissing her passionately before he vanished to where she knew not, but always leaving her body wanting more. If only the mist would clear and she could see his face?

Jane never did get to see the face of her rescuer, but his arms had felt so wonderful wrapped around her she'd wanted to stay locked in his embrace forever. She could hear his heart beating as furiously as her own as he'd held her close, and then, she would suddenly wake up: her heart beating twenty to the dozen, with the bed sheets wrapped around her heated body holding her captive. Every night she asked herself why she had such dreams. And what did they mean? Was it her subconscious telling her she needed to find someone she could fall in love with? Even so, she managed to convince herself she didn't have time to look for that one special man who would make her forget her career. Love, she'd long ago decided would have to wait. For her, second best wasn't on her agenda when it came to finding a husband. It had to be the real thing, or nothing; she had to be truly in love with the man *she* was to marry!

As the cross-country train drew into the country station the next morning, Jane could see her father waiting for her. Even from a distance she was shocked and disturbed by what she saw. He looked dishevelled and unkempt, which was unlike him. So different from the elegant man she'd known all her life. He appeared to have aged considerably as well, even though it had only been a few months since she'd last seen him. He no longer looked like the forty-eight-year-old he really was, but at least twenty years older. Even from a distance, she could see his complexion looked grey and haggard with deep worry lines etched on his face. Seeing him in the flesh, Jane wondered what could possibly have happened to bring about the changes she was witnessing. He appeared to be one-step away from looking like a "down and out". She felt angry, although she tried not to show her feelings as she greeted him with a hug. She was angry, not with him, but with herself. How could she have been so selfish and self-centred, putting her own life and career before him? Suddenly, she was racked with guilt, knowing her mother would never have forgiven her for neglecting him. Perhaps he was ill, after all? But when she stepped away from him she could see that wasn't the answer to what was wrong. It was something much deeper that he was trying to hide from her.

Taking his arm as they walked out of the station yard, Jane asked him how he was. Quite a normal question, for a concerned and loving daughter to ask, except, that Andrew was trying valiantly to be jovial with his answers. Jane could see his heart wasn't in it to be light hearted. Unlike other homecomings, when he would have swooped her up into his arms and twirled her around as he'd welcomed her home, this time he was holding onto her like an old man as they walked to where his car was parked.

The journey home down the country lanes seemed endless. They sat more or less in silence, her father neatly sidestepping her questions about his social life and the business. Curt and short answers were all she received from her gentle probing. His answers telling her nothing, except that by his very reticence she knew he was hiding something from her. She could sense that he definitely did have problems, but what were they? Did he have a life threatening illness? Was that his problem? She knew prying wasn't going to give her the answers she needed; she would have to be patient and give him time. Perhaps it was after all, her mother's death that was at the root of his problems and his depression. Losing her the cause of his downtrodden look, especially knowing how her parents had lived for each other, ever since they'd fallen in love as teenagers. This was the only explanation Jane could think of. But she was a determined young woman, and would make it her business to find out what was wrong, and then do something about it before she returned to London.

That first evening at home had seemed as endless as the journey from the station had been. After a light supper prepared and cooked by Jane, which in itself was unusual, as her father usually liked to show off his prowess in the kitchen; he'd finally escaped her quizzical glances by going into his study as soon as the meal was over, purposefully ignoring her as he closed the door behind him.

With her head full of questions she needed answering, Jane finally gave up and went to her old room where, after she'd mulled over her father's reluctance to talk, she fell asleep and where, yet again, and unbidden, she'd dreamt of the handsome and dashing pirate, saving her once more from some calamity, waking just as he'd been about to kiss her passionately. Oh, how she wanted her dream to continue, wanting him to go further and make love to her, her throbbing body leaving her desperately wanting fulfilment.

The next morning, as she waited in the kitchen for her father to appear for breakfast, she made a decision as to how best to proceed. She would try over the weekend to find out what it was that ailed him, even if it meant asking their family doctor, who was a personal friend of her father, to visit and examine him, to see if he was having a mental, or physical, breakdown, which is what Jane most feared might be about to happen!

Andrew kissed her lightly on the cheek in greeting, before sitting down at the table to eat what was put before him in silence. It wasn't until he'd finished, and had pushed his plate aside that he finally spoke, pre-empting Jane from her prepared line of questioning.

'Darling, I've tried hard not to bother you, but it's come to the point where I can't solve my problems on my own and, as it's to do with your inheritance, I think you need to know, as together we might find a solution?'

'What do you mean it's to do with my inheritance? And what,' she asked him calmly, even though she felt anything but calm, her stomach full of jittery butterflies, 'is it that I need to know?'

Pouring them both more coffee, she sat down opposite him determined not to get angry or upset. There was no point in getting uptight or aggressive knowing either emotion wouldn't solve her father's problem, whatever it was.

But surely, between them they could find a solution to anything untoward. Wasn't that something her mother had always instilled in her? A problem shared was a problem halved?

'It's the business! That's the problem!' Her father said slowly, spelling out his dilemma. 'Your inheritance! Financially the business is on its knees!'

Unable to fully comprehend what her father was saying, Jane asked him to explain. 'It's one of the best engineering factories in the country. It's always been the best, and certainly the most profitable! So what is it that has suddenly happened to change all of that?'

'It's entirely all my fault.' Andrew said, in a voice that was hardly audible.

'I failed to keep a tight rein on the finances. It didn't suddenly happen but I suppose I made an intrinsic mistake and should have known better! I trusted someone implicitly, believing him to be honourable and trustworthy. It was Tom Grainger! Do you remember him? He used to be my office manager. He'd always been honest and responsible for the day-to-day running of the factory and the accounts, but in just a few months, when I was at my lowest ebb and unfortunately not paying attention he systematically stole thousands and thousands of pounds from the company. It was so much money I doubt that the firm will ever recover!

'I was in such despair when I lost your mother I couldn't think straight: it was then he took advantage of my poor state of mind and fleeced the company. I didn't know it was happening, or even to what extent, until a few weeks ago. He'd kept it well hidden until, one Monday, he didn't turn up for work and I answered a call from a supplier asking when their outstanding accounts would be paid! It was then I checked the bank statements. It was all such a terrible shock and then the bank manager called me that same morning, confirming my worst fears. He told me they weren't going to extend my overdraft any longer as no payments had been made into the account! I couldn't believe what was happening.

'I'd never had an overdraft in my life! I've always had a dread of borrowing money. When I called in the auditors that same day they confirmed the company was virtually bankrupt. It was then I nearly died of shock! All this has happened within the last couple of months.

'The police are involved now, as I've had to press charges against Tom, not that they can do much about it as he's disappeared out of the country, along with the company's money. By the time the law catches up with him he will no doubt have spent it all and the business will probably have folded!'

Jane couldn't believe what she was hearing, or seeing, as she looked at her father, by now holding his head in his hands as he silently wept. She was looking at a broken man. The only other time she'd ever seen her father cry had been at the death of her mother. He'd always been the strong one in the family; competent in business and not given to panicking, he'd always been the rock on which she and her mother had relied.

His engineering company had been, and still was, one of the most respected in the country, making high quality products for the aero industry, all much in demand, but even that knowledge didn't help. If the suppliers weren't being paid, the company wouldn't be able to buy the materials it needed and getting credit while bankrupt would definitely not be an option. To add insult to injury, an unsympathetic bank manager had withdrawn its facilities from the company for the time being.

Jane could see what the problem was, but understanding what should be done now was an altogether different matter!

At least her degree in business studies had helped her to see the whole picture, and now she knew what they were up against she was going to be the one to come up with ideas on how the business could be saved.

'So what can I do to get us out of this mess?' she asked.

'There's nothing you can do, unless you've got hundreds of thousands of pounds sitting in your bank account you don't mind lending the company! The bank's already pulled the plug on us, so the company will have to go into liquidation any day soon. I can't see what else I can do. No one's very keen to loan money at the moment and no doubt the bank will insist on the business being sold so they can get some of their money back. It will then be broken up and sold piecemeal, unless there's someone out there willing to take it on; it's the ongoing finance that's the biggest problem. It's just a vicious circle.'

'I can't lay my hands on the huge amount of money you need,' Jane said, quietly, 'but there is one person who might be able to help!'

'And who,' her father asked, his eyebrows raised, 'might I ask is that?'

'My godfather, of course, that's who. Your old friend, Sir Ernest Miles! Go and see him and ask him for his advice. Also, don't forget he is a multimillionaire. He probably has more than you need in his piggy bank!'

'I'm not going to ask him for his personal money, that wouldn't be fair, but maybe you're right. I can always get his advice. I hadn't thought of him.'

It only took a few moments for Andrew to ring his friend and, for the rest of the weekend, Jane took advantage of having her father to herself and, once they'd discussed their options and exhausted all the angles and the why and wherefores of the company's problems, they began the task of sorting out some of her mother's treasures, a painful task they'd delayed doing for months.

But life has to go on and Andrew knew it was time for him to move on. Jane was right in getting him to make decisions that, until then, he'd been unable to even think about, let alone face.

Chapter Two

On the Monday morning Andrew went to see Sir Ernest Miles. The two men were old friends, their friendship going back to the early sixties, when they'd been growing up together in Yorkshire.

Sir Ernest's wife, Leah, and Isabel, Andrew's wife, had lived in the same Yorkshire town, in the same street of back-to-back houses near the mill where most of the people in the town worked. The women too had grown up together and were good friends; when they left school, they went to work in the mill and it was there, quite by chance at a social evening with friends that the two girls just happened to meet up with Andrew and Ernest and fall in love.

After a respectable three-year courtship, the two couples were quietly married on the same day, but in different churches. After the ceremonies, and a day trip to Ilkley moor for their honeymoons, they moved into rented rooms in the same old stone house in the city, sharing a minute kitchen and a newly installed bathroom.

Neither couple had anything very much in the way of worldly goods at this time, but what they did have was a deep and abiding love for each other and a burning ambition to do better than anyone else they'd grown up with.

It was one of the happiest times in their lives, even though, as they say in Yorkshire, '*they'd nowt, not so much as a brass farthing between them!*'

The newlyweds didn't care about possessions at the time, they weren't important. They had their love for each other and they all knew one-day the men would be successful and then they would be able to have everything they'd ever desired!

All this happened in the early seventies, at a time of unrest in the country, when unions dominated the factories and work became scarce throughout the land. Men had to work hard at whatever they could find to do, or live by their wits if they were to survive. Andrew and Ernest were just two men, amongst many thousands, young and old, struggling to make a living.

Fortunately, they were both wily and resourceful enough to get by, as well as willing to do whatever it took to feed, in Ernest's case, a growing brood of children. Jane hadn't been born yet, but when she did arrive in the eighties Andrew and Isabel were well established and thriving.

In their spare moments, Ernest and Andrew, would argue, good naturedly of course, as to which of them would be the first to become successful.

It was, as Andrew quite rightly suspected, Ernest. Of the two of them he was the most aggressive and what his brains couldn't get him his fists could.

For a short time, he became a boxer in his spare time, anything to earn extra money: being the right height and build for boxing, it was just one of the many means he used for earning extra money to fund his dreams.

Leah was always at his side and, whatever she lacked in bodily strength, she more than made up in business acumen; even so, she was more than glad when her husband's brains began to earn him more money than his fists!

Andrew meanwhile, had found his own niche in life. He'd gone into engineering, as an apprentice, where he'd learnt to use his hands, as well as his brains and, it wasn't long after he'd qualified he'd been made the manager at the engineering company where he'd learnt his trade.

The owner decided to retire a few years later and, not having sons to follow him into the business, he encouraged Andrew to buy the company. Andrew talked over this offer with Isabel who encouraged him to take on the business, helping him in the office for many years, in the meantime using the profits the business made over the next few years to help pay for the loan on the business, until, on the old man's death, Andrew found himself inheriting the company with his outstanding debt cancelled. It was from this lucky start he went on to do even greater things with the business, until this present fiasco, when his world, because of his complacency, had imploded!

In the meantime, the friendships between the two couples never wavered as Ernest and Andrew pursued each other up the ladder to success. It was only when they'd moved from out of the rented rooms and into their first houses their lives moved in different directions.

Andrew and Isabel eventually moved south, as Andrew chased his engineering dreams, while Ernest stayed put in Yorkshire where he eventually became the owner of a small paper and printing company; buying up smaller companies whenever he could. It was not only his and Leah's judicious management, but also Ernest's innate ability to know a good thing when he saw it that was the biggest contributor to his success. Finally, he became the owner of a hugely successful conglomerate of companies that was to see him getting a knighthood several years later for his efforts. It was then, only a few years later, that he too finally moved away from his beloved Yorkshire to the south of England, to be near his new business headquarters, settling into a large house in a village, not far from where Andrew and Isabel lived.

It was Ernest's fond hope the nearness of Isabel, Leah's old friend, would salve her heartache at having to leave her latest grandchild in Yorkshire but, the saddest part for Leah was, after having spent so many years missing her dearest friend, she became heartbroken, when only a year or so later, Isabel died and she found herself living in a part of England for which she had no affection with hardly any true friends.

Andrew and Ernest were alike in many ways both being gruff Yorkshire men, more inclined to plain speaking; and very forthright in their views, both believing in calling a spade a spade.

That Monday morning, after they'd exchanged pleasantries and greetings in Ernest's light and airy sitting room, adjacent to his office, and their coffee cups had been refilled, they started to discuss Andrew's problems at great length, in the only way they both knew; straight to the point, with no messing about and with no holds barred. Andrew began to relax as he told his old friend the whole story and, after a while Ernest knew everything there was to know about his old friend's sorry predicament.

Of course, Sir Ernest was absolutely shocked by what he'd learnt, understanding the damage brought about by an employee Andrew had once trusted, knowing from his own business that being diligent was a requirement needed to keep any company safe. He knew from his own experience it didn't pay to be too trusting.

Sir Ernest's heart went out to his friend for, like Jane, he too believed it had been the death of Isabel that was probably the main reason for the perpetrator getting away with his crime. He was even more shocked when Andrew told him the scale of the theft. He sat and thought, his fingers entwined and steepled as he mulled over the problems facing his friend and the options he now faced. For a while, he said nothing, aware any advice he gave might not be in time to save the company, until he had a sudden thought as the name, Jake Adams, came into his mind.

Jake Adams, he knew was definitely the ideal man. He was the one person who might possibly be able to save Andrew's company. He was well known and trusted in the city as a "business angel". Someone who not only bought into a company and financed it but managed it as well, working alongside the owners as the company was put back onto its feet.

Apart from being known as a "business angel" there were other less complimentary names Jake Adams was called in the city, all impolite, but Sir Ernest chose not to disclose those to Andrew, who was very apprehensive of such a plan when Ernest first suggested it to him.

Even if he could find someone else prepared to buy into the company, it would still mean he would lose control of it, but Sir Ernest begged him to stop and think, pleading with his old friend to act sensibly and not allow his emotions to determine his actions. This of course was easier said than done, but Andrew knew he needed someone prepared to invest a huge sum of money in his company and how many men were there in the country who would be prepared to risk such an amount without having the most say?

Sir Ernest left Andrew alone to think over his proposition while he went into his office see to his own business. When he walked back into the room an hour later, he smiled and shook his head. Andrew had fallen asleep in the chair, exhaustion and worry finally taking their hold. It was some time before he woke, just as his old friend again walked back into the room.

'Sorry about that! I must have dozed off.' He said, not realising he'd slept for a couple of hours.

'No problem, you looked as though you needed to sleep. I don't suppose you've had many nights when you've slept properly since you found out you were in danger of losing all you'd worked for?'

'Yes, you're right, of course. It's been a terrible time. And the worst part was telling Jane. Thank goodness she's got a sensible head on her shoulders and understands business. I should have told her right from the beginning. But I didn't. I suppose it was my pride getting in the way. Anyway, I've been thinking. Perhaps it would be a good idea if I contacted your man and had a few words with him?'

'Leave it to me. I'll give him a call and fix a day, time and place where you can meet.'

With that, Sir Ernest went into his office, where Andrew could hear him on the phone making arrangements: within a few minutes, he'd been set up to meet the young businessman who he hoped would turn out to be his company's saviour.

The meeting wasn't going to happen for another week as the young man had to go to Italy on business, but he'd promised Sir Ernest he would call Andrew as soon as he returned home. This delay caused Andrew to worry, until he realised he wouldn't be able to find anyone else before then in any case, so worrying seemed to be a pointless exercise.

By the time he returned home, Jane had completed clearing out cupboards and drawers that hadn't been touched since her mother's death.

She'd spent the day sorting through several boxes that held old albums of photographs and letters her mother had kept for years. It was therefore, paradoxically, both a happy time and yet a sad one, as she relived memories of her childhood, glad to have done it, as it was one chore her father had been putting off for the past year.

Jane could see from the look on her father's face when he arrived home that his state of mind had improved, even in such a short time. He seemed more optimistic and relaxed than earlier and even appeared to have lost some of the worry lines he'd had before his meeting with her godfather, perhaps it was the knowledge there was a young entrepreneur in the city, who, hopefully, was going to help him financially that had helped.

Of course, Andrew failed to tell Jane any financial help he received would probably come with strings attached and, as it was her birthright he was fighting to get back, he felt a little ashamed at his deception, but he was prepared to do anything to keep the company afloat, not only for his own financial gain, but to keep his loyal workforce employed.

The next morning, Jane went back to London, but only after eliciting a promise from her father that he would phone and let her know as soon as he'd talked to Jake Adams. She also told him, in no uncertain terms that she wanted to be involved in all negotiations regarding the business, to which Andrew reluctantly agreed, but which he knew was inevitable, given what had happened.

A week later, Andrew finally met up for the first time with Jake Adams. It was a difficult first meeting, caused mainly by Andrew's embarrassment at what he saw as him having to grovel for help from such a young man, but it only took a few minutes for Andrew to realise Jake Adams was indeed the brightest young man he'd ever encountered. More than that, Andrew liked him, as a man, and as a businessman, especially when Jake told him how he'd become so rich and in such a relatively short time. Andrew could see Sir Ernest Miles description of the young man had been spot on! He was a young man of steel and, even though he was young, he was also arrogant and no doubt very aggressive in his business dealings; not traits Andrew shared, but admired in others, it just wasn't his way of working but, given he was the one whose company was nearly bankrupt, he thought perhaps he ought to acquire some of Jake Adams's traits!

Jake, thankfully, had grasped Andrew's problems straightaway, putting him instantly at his ease as he told him honestly he would help and even how he intended to do this, if what he was proposing was acceptable to Andrew.

Mainly, any decision he made to finance the company would see him in charge and that for the time being Andrew would be his second in command. That wasn't how Andrew had envisaged the deal, but he had to think of the men who worked for him. They came first and, as Jake Adams was a busy man with many interests, abroad as well at home in Britain, Andrew didn't think he would get too much interference. But this was only one part to how Jake Adams worked, as Andrew was to find out.

The two men spent some considerable time discussing the pros and cons of how to make the company profitable again, and how much Jake was prepared to invest. When Andrew told him he wanted Jake to meet his daughter, as any decisions made must be ratified with her, Jake Adams said nothing; his raised eyebrows telling Andrew much more than any words could ever have said! Jake obviously didn't like women in business, especially when it came to his deals!

And so it came about that a couple of days later Jane went to meet the company's saviour. It was at this meeting she'd walked into her father's office and met Jake Adams for the first time. More importantly, had she known at the time, it was the day her destiny was finally revealed!

That first meeting had been charged with sexual tension, hers, and Jake's. Their sexual interest in each other apparent even to Andrew, but had left them both wondering just exactly what it was that had happened. They'd been mesmerised by each other; so much so, Jake found it hard to concentrate on the business deal he was about to broker with her father. His only thought; he had to escape from the confines of Andrew's office and get his mind back onto business rather than his thoughts on how quickly he could get Jane Reynolds out of her sexy high heels and business suit, and into his bed!

Once he'd left the office, with not only his briefcase bulging, Jane had nervously laughed, shaking her head in her bemusement. She couldn't believe what had taken place, neither could she believe how her emotions had surfaced to such an extent that she'd wanted to race after Jake Adams and beg him to take her to bed and have his wicked way with her, right there and then!

There was something about him her body instantly recognised, even though she was quite sure they'd never met before.

'So what was that all about?' she'd asked her father rather ruefully, trying to hide her embarrassment from him as the outer door closed and she'd heard Jake's car purr into life.

Unlike Jane, Andrew had been able to interpret Jake's body language. It was a man thing!

The minute Jane had walked into the room the young man seemed to have changed. Suddenly he'd gone from being a confident and arrogant businessman he'd first met, one able to make split second decisions, to one whose mind had suddenly turned to mush, and all because his daughter had appeared.

Jane might not have known what had happened, but Andrew did. He'd seen a young man falling headlong into love. As regards to Jane's feelings? He wasn't a hundred per cent sure, but he thought she might have been struck by the same thunderbolt as Jake, except she hadn't as yet realised it!

That same evening, Jane's best friend, Sylvie phoned, inviting Jane, and Andrew, to a nearby country house hotel for a celebratory meal. She was still recovering from the birth of her second child, but knowing Jane would have to be back in London the next day, and with her husband, Leo, returning to America a few days later, she'd decided Leo should take Jane and Andrew out for the meal.

The hotel she'd chosen was noted for its superb cuisine and, that evening it had excelled, making a special evening even more so, especially for Andrew, who'd confessed to Jane and Leo he'd had no social life since he'd lost Isabel.

They were just about to leave the hotel when Jane stumbled, and would have fallen, had Leo not grabbed hold of her waist and held onto her tightly, just as Jake Adams happened to walk into the foyer with a beautiful young woman hanging onto his arm.

He looked stunned for a moment as he recognised Jane and then he saw Leo's arm around her waist. He'd glowered at them both with such intensity it caused Jane to stifle a nervous laugh, his venomous look taking her by surprise. For a moment or two she was speechless. She was just about to speak and introduce Leo when, to her surprise, he walked away without giving her the chance, the expression on his face one she couldn't fathom at all.

Leo on the other hand was highly amused and intrigued by the incident, as he'd realised immediately the man, whoever he was, had been overcome with jealousy. Trying to hide his amusement, Leo wondered when Jane had met the man and, more to the point, who the devil was he?

Andrew, of course, had missed meeting his young saviour, as he'd been in the cloakroom, but later, when Jane told him what had happened, he wasn't as much in the dark as Jane thought, knowing only too well why Jake had acted as he did; it was jealousy at seeing her with another man! If only he'd told Jane then, that when a man falls in love he becomes territorial, no other male is allowed near the woman he's selected as his mate! As for Jane, she was curious to know the name of the attractive young woman hanging onto Jake's arm, no doubt hanging onto his every word?

Neither Jake, nor Jane, slept well that evening. Both of them consumed with thoughts of each other. Jake's were jealous thoughts, of course. As for Jane, even her erotic dream and the passionate antics of her pirate who'd suddenly taken on an uncanny resemblance to Jake Adams, did little to uplift her spirits.

The next morning, Jane returned to London, with her father's promise he would be in touch ringing in her ears just as soon as he heard from Jake with his proposals for the business: she could do no more than kiss him goodbye at the station, with a feeling of impending doom inside her. Why, she asked herself, did she feel that way? She'd only met the wretched man once and for no more than five minutes, but in that short time he'd created havoc with her feelings. They'd had no conversation, and then, the second time she'd seen him, he'd looked at her with such loathing she wondered what she'd done to make him feel that way? Why did he dislike her so much? And, would his dislike of her have an adverse effect on her father's business? Jane tried to shrug off her feelings, deciding when her father called with the date and time of the meeting, she would confront the arrogant Jake Adams, face to face, and ask him to explain just exactly what his problem was?

Jake, in the meantime, knew only too well what his problem was, but how to solve it was another matter. He knew he was emotionally cold! His emotions locked inside him and had been, ever since his parents had divorced when he'd been eight years old and he'd been separated from his mother.

He'd been sent away to a boarding school, as his father had demanded; not prepared for any other man who might happen to fall in love with his ex-wife, to rear his son!

Boarding schools are alien environments for all children, but especially for a sensitive and loving little boy like Jake; strangely enough, he survived his Spartan schooling, and years later even he agreed his upbringing and education was probably responsible for his cold-hearted personality. Over the years, he'd learnt to keep his emotions under control, hiding them away as he aged and the more successful he'd become.

He'd managed to use this cold-hearted persona to his advantage, and not only in his business deals, but also in the few relationships he'd had with women, who, by and large, were attracted to him by his good looks, his wealth being a genuine bonus.

Jake knew it would take someone very special to thaw his emotions, so, on the morning Jane had walked into her father's office, he knew immediately he'd found the perfect woman to defrost him. His only problem was how could he get her to feel the same way about him?

Seeing her with Leo, and thinking he was Jane's lover made Jake rethink his strategy as to how he should help Andrew Reynolds and, for once, the fates were on his side, but for the time being they weren't telling what they had in store for him!

Chapter Three

There was a backlog of work waiting for Jane when she walked into the office. It took until mid-afternoon before her in-tray was empty and the problems that had stockpiled in her absence had been solved.

Jessie fielded the calls, until four o'clock, when an urgent call from the company chairman came through that only Jane could take care of.

The call was for her to carry out a special training assignment in New York. It was short notice but she had to take over immediately from a sick colleague and, as that was the nature of her work, she knew she had to leave the office and get ready. She was used to leaving Jessie in charge and, once she was booked onto the early morning flight to New York, she rushed back to her flat to pack.

Jane had put her thoughts of Jake Adams on hold, but as she tried to sleep that night she could see him quite clearly. It was his eyes that first came to her mind.

No, that wasn't strictly true, she'd been intrigued by his eyes of course, but it was how he'd looked in his business suit that had really caught her attention. It took very little effort now for her to imagine how he would look when he wasn't wearing it. The very thought of him being naked aroused her as she brought this image of him to the forefront of her mind. Then, the thought of him, lying next to her in bed, made her nipples rise and her heart start to beat really fast as she imagined them, lying together, both naked of course: caressing each other, until she could stand it no longer and tried to think of other things but it was impossible. She longed for him. She wanted him to kiss her with his perfect lips, imagining what he would be doing to her with his hands. It was all too much; her emotions were on such a high she felt tears of frustration falling onto her cheeks as her body cried out for him, knowing he wasn't the man for her. It looked as though he was already spoken for with the young woman who'd been looking up at him with such adoration.

Although she was twenty-five years old, Jane was not given to sleeping around, but then neither was she sorry she was no longer a virgin. She'd happily lost her virginity years ago, aged eighteen, while she'd been away at university where she'd met a young man. Being young, innocent and inexperienced, there'd been lots of exciting moments as they explored each other's bodies. Lots of kissing, with her young man nipping her nipples and caressing her breasts before the fumbling moments when he'd reached down to explore the contents of her underwear, where finally they made what to them both was a big step towards being adults, and did the deed.

Unfortunately, that first time wasn't a happy occasion for Jane. It had been messy and certainly not fulfilling, although the young man seemed happy enough to have bedded the most attractive woman in the university; as for Jane, she preferred not to think about what had happened. It was only afterwards, when she came across the perfect book that explained, in words and pictures, just what she and any young man who took her fancy should do to make lovemaking a satisfactory experience for them both.

For the rest of her university years, there'd been another young man who'd found his way into her bed and, for a while, she'd enjoyed his company, and his body, until she realised he wanted a relationship that would give him a temporary wife; one who would do the cooking and cleaning, as well as a convenient live-in lover for when it suited him. After a while Jane decided she didn't want such a relationship, realising she was far too young to be no more than a young man's skivvy and, more importantly, her examination results were far more important than looking after a man who was quite capable of doing for himself. She'd therefore finished the relationship and, ever since, she'd been much more circumspect in her choice of young men, making a point of not encouraging them to have feelings for her, which was quite difficult considering her looks and bubbly personality.

Once qualified, with a degree in management and economics and happily working at her first job, her social life fell pretty much to zero! Except, of course for the office parties she had to attend, deciding she was much too busy and serious about her future for frivolous relationships.

It even got to the point where her mother told her she needed to find herself a young man and settle down, or she would turn out to be an old maid. This had made Jane laugh and, up to her meeting with Jake Adams, she'd had no interest in men at all, and certainly had no intention of settling down to marriage and motherhood for some years to come. How little we know of what the fates have decided for us! Or even what is our destiny!

Suddenly, she sat up in bed. Was Jake Adams the elusive man from the tarot cards? For the life of her she couldn't understand why she found him so attractive. He was the antithesis of the type of man she was normally attracted to.

First of all, he was arrogant and rude, if his behaviour in her father's office and at the hotel when he saw her with Leo was an indication of his normal way of behaving. He definitely wasn't her type at all. She didn't go for the debonair, man-about-town types. Oh, and then there were his eyes that had stared at her with such intensity: amber eyes that looked like a wild animal! And how he'd stared at her, stripping her naked with his gaze, as though she was destined to be his dinner.

Had she been younger, and still a virgin, she would have been scared of him, but then she realised, that's exactly how she had felt. She was scared, but not of him, but at the intensity of the feelings of lust she'd felt, but why, when he wasn't her type?

It was a mad scramble the next morning to be ready and at the airport in time for her flight to America. Lustful dreams of Jake had woken her early and had led to her caressing her own body, until she'd climaxed, leaving her exhausted.

It wasn't until the plane had taken off and the flight was well under way she'd finally begun to relax and took out the book she intended to read. She'd hardly read more than a couple of pages of the latest blockbuster when her eyes had closed and, with the book lying open on her lap, she'd slept most of the way across the Atlantic.

After checking into her hotel, just a few blocks away from the training venue, and after taking a quick shower, she was ready to do what she was good at, training others.

And that's how Jane's days flew by, until the night before she was due to return to London, when she'd been invited by her colleagues to join them in an evening out. To her surprise, as she entered the restaurant, she suddenly saw Leo, Sylvie's husband, also on business in New York and dining on his own. Thrilled to see her, he agreed to join her and her colleagues for the evening. He was such good company he managed to take her mind away, for the time being at least, from Jake and his scowling good looks as she'd last seen him at the hotel with his ladylove on his arm!

Leo is the Financial Director for a global company and frequently travels back and forth across the Atlantic and, when he found Jane was returning to England the next day, and after comparing flight times, he surprised her by telling her he would be on the same plane and would arrange for them to be seated together.

Jane liked Leo enormously, ever since he'd fallen in love with Sylvie, her best friend, while they'd all been at the same university. When they'd all qualified, he'd proposed to Sylvie and she'd accepted. Jane was chosen as her maid of honour, and now was godmother to their two young children, a girl, Louisa, five-years old and already a beautiful replica of Sylvie, and the new baby, Anton who followed his father for his good looks.

It was a mutual liking as Leo admired Jane too. He thought her to be, after Sylvie, the most beautiful and intelligent young woman he'd ever met and hoped one day she would meet a man, equally as intelligent, one who would fall in love with her and appreciate her for far more than her looks.

Even though he loved Sylvie, and couldn't wait to get home to her and the children, for once, Leo looked forward to the long flight home and sharing a few hours with Jane, whose company he knew would improve the journey home enormously.

Their flight arrived at Heathrow on time. Having arranged to travel into the city together, Leo hailed a taxi from the rank. He was just in the process of opening the door and helping Jane in, when his eye was caught by a black limousine drawing up behind them and then at the man just getting out. He looked familiar and was obviously in a hurry to head into the terminal until suddenly he caught sight of Leo staring at him. Jake recognised him although not from where. At the same time, he saw Jane, partially hidden by Leo's bulk. The smile he'd been about to give him changed into a scowl of pure rage, as it suddenly dawned on him how he knew him! For a moment, Leo was baffled as to why this man's expression should have changed so quickly, then, thinking Jane might want to acknowledge the man, he touched her arm and pointed in Jake's direction. As she turned her head at Leo's touch, so she saw Jake. Her heart lurched in her chest. For a minute or to, she felt light headed, collapsing onto the back seat of the taxi only managing a weak smile at him, but Jake merely nodded at her in acknowledgement: his mouth contorted into a grimace that led her to believe he too might have been in pain, until she saw the final look he gave Leo. It was the same glowering look he'd given him at the hotel. Without further ado, and with a final glance at Jane that left her gasping at its ferocity, Jake Adams went storming into the airport.

As their taxi headed towards the city, Jane was at a loss to know what to say to Leo. She felt as though her heart had been clutched from her body and squeezed dry of its blood.

How could she explain Jake's behaviour, when she didn't understand it herself? As for Leo, he couldn't understand what had happened either to cause Jane's obvious distress at seeing the angry young man. He was puzzled. What could he say that wouldn't be an intrusion?

Until she gave him an explanation, all he could do was to hold her hand and talk to her in the soft tones he used to comfort his own small daughter when she'd fallen down and hurt herself. How he wished Sylvie were with him. She would have known immediately what to do and say that would alleviate her friend's pain. He would have to tell her what had happened and let her make of it what she would, as for once Leo was totally baffled!

The rest of the week rushed by for Jane as she tried to catch up with her work and write up her notes for the chairman on how the training schedule had gone in America.

Her father had left a message with Jessie that he'd heard from Jake Adams and a meeting had been arranged for the following Monday. At the mention of Jake's name, Jane's heart started to beat faster and, for a moment, she felt faint, such was the effect he had on her.

The meeting was to be held in a small room at Andrew's club, where he planned on staying overnight. But what Andrew failed to tell her, was that Jake had already put a proposition to him that would ensure the company's future, swearing him to secrecy, until he'd met Jane and told her himself.

Andrew, was secretly worried by Jake's proposal and, knowing time was running out, he had no other option but to agree to Jake's terms, if the company was to survive intact. He had to accept what was being offered, but would Jane agree to Jake's outlandish demand and, if not, what would happen next?

Oblivious to what lay ahead, Jane arrived at Andrew's club on time, her heart beating twenty to the dozen, which seemed to happen every time she thought of Jake.

The door to the meeting room was slightly ajar and, with a terrible sense of foreboding, Jane pushed it open and walked in to find her father and Jake waiting for her. With her heart in her mouth, she felt like an animal walking into a trap. She desperately wanted to turn tail and run but she knew that wasn't an option. She had to stay and listen to the plans Jake had made; plans she hoped would save her father's company from ruination, but something inside her told her she wasn't going to like what she was about to hear.

Jane quite expected to see Jake with a frown on his handsome face but instead, she saw the face she'd dreamt of the night before and this time with a smile of welcome on his well-shaped lips: lips that in her dreams she'd kissed passionately. Suddenly, she felt uneasy, as though she'd already been captured and ensnared, knowing there was nothing she could do, other than to let what was about to happen, happen!

'Hello, Jane,' Jake said silkily, holding out his hand to take the one she cautiously offered. A big change, from how he'd reacted when he'd last seen her at the airport.

'Hello Jake,' was all she managed to say; her mouth too dry with nerves to say more. She shook his proffered hand then quickly dropped it, afraid to hang onto it and instinctively moving closer to her father, who took her in his arms and kissed her in greeting.

No one spoke for a few moments, the air so full of tension, until they were seated at the table, where a tray of coffee had been set ready for them.

Suddenly, feeling cold, Jane felt herself shiver, her body's defence mechanism to her rising stress levels taking over.

She sat down at the table and tried to recover her composure. Andrew joined her, leaving Jake to remove some papers from his briefcase. Picking up one sheet at random he started to study it at length.

After a while he cleared his throat and looked directly at Jane, taking in the two glittering jewels that shone from out of her pale face. He could see she was anxious, aware of her fear he lowered his gaze to her full and generous mouth, set in an uncharacteristic straight line. Holding her head high, keeping her posture upright, Jane stared back at him.

'I've come to a conclusion as to what needs to be done to solve your father's problem!' Jake said in a commanding tone of voice that defied any argument from Jane or her father.

Looking first at Andrew, who he could also see looked nervous, then quickly at Jane. Jake continued.

'I've already spoken to your father and he's agreed with me that the solution I'm about to propose will be in the best interests of the company…' He stopped speaking for a few moments, looking directly at Andrew, who by now was looking decidedly, guilty, as well as nervous.

He then stared at Jane, perched demurely on the edge of her seat, impatient for him to tell her his proposal to save the company.

'My suggestion is…' Jake hesitated, 'that I will take over the business and pay off all its debts…' again he stopped in mid-sentence, staring straight at her, 'on condition…' pausing now for his next words to have their full impact and effect on Jane, 'that you marry me straight away!'

Jane's head shot up, her eyes looking straight into Jake's. The expression on her face said it all. She thought he'd lost leave of his senses, that he was quite mad and then, when she looked at her father, she thought the same of him!

Her head was spinning as she realised exactly what it was that Jake had just said. Suddenly, she felt as though a hundred hammers were banging against her brain. Whatever was the matter with the man? Marry him to save her father's business? Never, not in a million years!

But she said nothing. She felt powerless to give vent to her feelings. She looked across at her father who was studiously avoiding her eyes and then she looked at Jake, but his face was impassive, giving no sign as to his thoughts.

But her thoughts were obvious. Jake Adams could see for himself she thought him to be a complete lunatic and that he should be locked up, and the key thrown away. Why did he think she would even contemplate his outlandish proposal? Suddenly she felt an indubitable compulsion to get out of the room, the only problem, her legs wouldn't move! She was incapable of standing up, let alone run! She felt trapped! Minutes ticked by without as much as a breath to be heard, until Andrew began to speak, breaking the heavy silence, then to Jane's utter chagrin, and in a pleading voice, her father quietly urged her to accept Jake's marriage proposal.

It suddenly became quite clear that Jake had somehow managed to blackmail her father, obviously telling him he would refuse to bail out the company if she refused his generous offer of marriage, thus forcing the business to close, which in turn would leave all the workforce jobless! Not only had he blackmailed her father, he was now doing the same to her.

Her dilemma? She would be the one responsible for all the misery the workforce would have to endure if she refused and, as there was no one else her father could turn to, it was up to her to save the company! It was as desperate as that.

'What about me?' She'd cried inwardly. 'What about my life?'

Marriage to Jake Adams hadn't been part of her plan for the future. She might have dreamt about him, but as for marriage! That was another thing altogether and in any case, why would he want to marry her? He didn't know anything about her and, come to think of it, what did she know about him? He might look handsome and sexy, but surely, there had to be something more than just being sexually attracted to someone before getting married, or, was she, like Jake Adams, living in "cloud cuckoo land"?

Jake let Jane do her thinking while he poured the coffee, holding out a cup towards her. It took a mighty effort on her part not to take it, as her desire at that moment was to fling it all over him. How dare he presume to think she would marry him, just to save her father's failing business! As for her father, what could she say about him? He seemed quite happy to arrange a marriage between herself and Jake Adams as being the solution to his problems, without any consideration for her feelings. As far as she was concerned, he was acting just like a pimp!

Ignoring the coffee, Jane picked up a glass of water that was on the table in front of her that she sipped instead, relishing its coolness. The cool water going some way to calming the inner turmoil raging within her. Then, with no comment to either man, she stood up, a trifle unsteadily, as she gathered up her handbag and made to leave the room in as dignified manner as she could.

Jake suddenly realised she was about to flee and hurried to the door, reaching it just a shade before her, blocking her exit and then, taking hold of her arm, he spoke quietly, out of earshot of her father, his voice low and tender. 'I'd like to marry you very much,' he said, 'and it wouldn't be a marriage of convenience. I'd want us to have a "proper" marriage!'

Jane was dumbfounded. Whatever did this madman think he was saying? He must be even madder than she'd first thought to even think she would listen to what he was saying, let alone agree to it, or even be willing to accept him as her husband, just to save her father from financial ruin. It was an outlandish suggestion and one she didn't intend taking seriously!

She shrugged his arm away, making no comment at his words, not even giving him a backward glance as she opened the door and stormed out of the room, leaving Jake to return to her father, making the cryptic comment. 'Well, that went well, I think!'

By the time she reached her flat, Jane had managed to calm down a little. Instead of being really angry, now she just seethed, at both men, but at one in particular, her father, sure in her own mind he'd colluded with Jake in persuading her to marry him; done not for her benefit, but to save his business and, no matter what he said or did, this wasn't the time when fathers made decisions as to whom their daughters should marry. This was the twenty-first century for goodness sake, not the Dark ages, and she would choose her own husband, thank you very much!

Chapter Four

Jake reluctantly watched as Jane walked away from him. All he wanted was to take her in his arms and kiss her, for he really was a man in love. Jane wasn't like any woman he'd ever known before and he knew he needed her in his life to become complete as a person. He needed her love. Her leaving had only increased his determination to have her as his wife, stubbornly refusing to believe he couldn't teach her how to love him. As he turned back into the room he could tell from Andrew's expression he was just as upset at Jane's outright refusal to consider his marriage proposal as he was. But what Andrew could really see, was his backer vanishing into the mist and his company folding, especially if Jane didn't change her mind and agree to become Jake's wife. He also knew her well; she was high-spirited and feisty, as well as being fiercely independent, a fact Jake obviously hadn't yet fully realised and neither was she a woman easily impressed with the trappings of wealth; nor would she be enamoured by a marriage proposal that had strings attached, such as the one Jake had given her. Andrew knew her independent streak came from her mother, as did the romantic notions of wanting to be wooded and courted.

If Jake had really fallen in love, the sooner he approached her in a more loving way the better. Perhaps, Andrew thought to himself, he should have a few words with his prospective son-in-law and put him on the right track! But before he could even begin to formulate such a speech in his mind, Jake had gathered up the remaining papers and, after shuffling them into some semblance of order, he stowed them quickly into his briefcase and snapped it shut. The next minute, with his hand outstretched, he faced Andrew and bade him farewell, a wry grimace on his face.

'I'm sorry,' he said, as he walked towards the door with Andrew. 'I didn't handle that very well, did I?'

Andrew patted the young man on the arm in a fatherly manner, for he liked Jake. He seriously thought he would make Jane a good husband, even though he did have a few rough edges that needed smoothing. In the meantime, Jake had to improve his courtship technique if he was to win his fair lady, but at that moment, Andrew didn't quite know how to advise him in that department!

'Don't worry,' he told Jake, 'I'm going to see her later, I'll put in a good word for you, I'll even go so far as to tell her she could no better than to accept your offer!'

Jake laughed, rather cynically. 'Fine, I'll leave it with you then?' Knowing full well if Andrew knew which side his bread was buttered he had to get Jane to agree to his marriage proposal, regardless of whether she loved him or not if the business was to survive and, with that, Jake left the room leaving Andrew with his mind in a turmoil and full of anxiety. As for the fates, they didn't care. They had other things to do.

As much as he wanted Jane to be his wife, Jake knew he'd have to wait and see what happened over the next day or two. First of all, though, he would send her flowers. He remembered his mother saying years ago most women could be wooed by flowers, perhaps, Jake suddenly thought, he ought to call his mother and ask her advice but, as soon as the thought came into his mind he dismissed it; his courtship of Jane Reynolds was one subject not open for discussion with anyone, other than the lady in question. And, until they were safely married, he didn't intend for his family to even know she existed!

How to not only catch a woman, but then to keep her, was going to be a whole new learning experience for Jake. He'd never been in love before, neither had he done any serious chasing, as all his past conquests had been with women more flattered by his wealth and power, than by his looks or charm; learning how to convince the one woman he wanted to spend the rest of his life with was certainly going to be a new challenge; a learning curve for Jake Adams that was long overdue.

Although Jane might have gained the impression Jake was experienced in the ways of women and love, it was untrue. He also knew he had a lot to change, and quickly, if he was ever going to win her heart and hand, finally knowing there was much more to bedding a woman like Jane than he could ever have imagined. But Jake was an intelligent young man, having graduated with a top economics degree from the best university in America, to which he'd won a full scholarship at the age of eighteen. Then afterwards, when he'd spent a couple of years working on Wall Street, gaining practical experience, before returning to England where he'd been head-hunted by one of the "big five" companies.

In his enthusiasm to succeed in business, he'd sadly neglected to learn the skills needed to become a good husband and father, consequently, he knew very little, in fact practically nothing, about the art of courtship. Oh! Yes! He knew how to get a woman into his bed and make love to her, or least have sex, which is quite different and, in the past, there had been many women who would have loved to have married him; unfortunately, Jake never met one he'd had the slightest inclination to marry, and neither did he have to pursue a woman, married or single to get her into his bed; it was his wealth that was his main attraction to women, exactly as bees are attracted to nectar!

Jake was now aware in the past that he'd been selfish, toying with a woman's emotions and at last his conscience troubled him; pricking him into being ashamed at how he'd used women as mere sexual objects and then, once they'd satisfied him, discarding them without a seconds thought. He knew he had to change, or he would lose the one woman he desperately wanted.

Once he'd amassed the first of his many millions, Jake started in earnest to invest serious money in enterprises others wouldn't look at, until suddenly, he found he could do no wrong; he had the magical "Midas" touch where money was concerned and, as the money poured in, with such apparent ease his fellow professionals became envious. It was at this point he saw his future lay in buying businesses that were failing. He would then inject them with money and any new technical help available and turn them around and then, when they were profitable again, he would sell them and make even more money. Sometimes he even bought businesses that were beyond his help, it was then he fell easily into "asset stripping", which earned him the nickname "that bloody pirate" by those in the city; businessmen who were disgruntled by his cut throat methods, but Jake didn't care what his colleagues, or his enemies had to say.

Being a law unto himself, he enjoyed the power having money gave him, even though he knew something was lacking in his life and then, when he first saw Jane, he'd stopped, long enough to think about it, and knew what it was he lacked; it was a proper home life, something he hadn't had as a youngster and that was probably at the root of his driving ambition and his selfishness. It was his parents divorcing when he'd been very young that had had an adverse effect on his view on marriage and family life, even though both his mother and father had happily remarried and had other children he was quite close to them but he still blamed his parents for sending him away to boarding school, thus depriving him of a family life of his own. (A fact even they acknowledged years later to be a truism.)

Jake's new siblings, a half-sister, Sara, from his mother's new marriage and a half brother, Daniel, from his father's were, of course, many years younger and while they were small children, he saw little of them, as he was either away at school or in college, or abroad. It wasn't until he was in his late twenties, and they were teenagers, he'd got to know them, by which time he'd become the attractive much older brother, with his own flat in Chelsea that had easy access to all the theatres and museums in the city. They visited him as often as his work commitments would allow, and soon he became a convenient minder when his parents wanted time alone. It was then the two youngsters came to know and admire their older brother.

It didn't particularly bother Jake having them to stay for they were an interesting pair and he liked them both. Daniel was definitely the smart one out of his two siblings and even Jake could see traits in the boy that reminded him perhaps a little of himself at the same age. Sara was different though, being the beauty of the family, taking after his mother for looks.

It had been Sara, the attractive young lady Jane had seen hanging onto Jake's arm, the night she'd been at the hotel with her father and Leo, the night when Jake had looked at her in such a scathing manner and Leo knew he'd seen a man disappointed in love!

Jake loved living in the city and especially his Chelsea apartment, more for the convenience of where it was in relation to the capital's nightlife, but after falling in love with Jane, his thoughts suddenly changed. He'd decided they would have to have the sort of home suitable to raise the children in, because he knew he wanted to have children with Jane. It would have to be somewhere peaceful though, in a small village, yet not too distant from the city. All he had to do was to convince Jane to marry him!

Until his first meeting with her, Jake had been a man-about-town, with absolutely no inclination to smell country air, let alone live there, him being a committed city dweller, but all that changed the morning she walked into her father's office in her sassy business suit and her sexy high heeled shoes and, for the first time in his life, Jake had been completely bowled over. She was the most beautiful woman he'd ever seen. He was so completely smitten he no longer cared what it would cost him to bankroll her father's ailing company, just as long as he could have her! Unfortunately for Jake, Jane Reynolds wasn't going to be the easy pushover his other conquests had been. This was one lady he wasn't going to find it easy to get into his bed! His wealth made no impression on her at all.

What he needed he knew, was a plan of action if he was to win her over, a business plan and, the first item on the plan would be how to woo her if he was to win his fair lady!

The first salvo in his campaign of wooing Jane took the form of a bouquet of long stemmed red roses, all beautifully wrapped in fancy cellophane and tied with a huge red bow, delivered to her door within an hour of her returning home. The card attached might have begged her forgiveness for his crass behaviour, but the underlying message was still quite clear, he was determined to pursue her and persuade her to marry him, leaving her in no doubt this was just the first round of fire in the battle, but who would win?

Now Jane had a dilemma? She wasn't used to receiving such large and lavish bouquets, the perfume of which filled her small flat until suddenly, she started to mellow, just a little, as she buried her face in the lush blooms.

Although she thought Jake to be the most arrogant and abrasive man she'd ever met, to her discomfort, her heart lurched every time she thought of him. She'd started to feel her mind set and resolve weakening the more her physical desire for him took over from her common sense.

'Please,' she'd prayed to her unseen God, 'don't let me fall too much in love with him!' But it was too late, the deed was done, her God, and the fates, had merely smiled, ignoring her request, for they had plans for her and Jake Adams.

Back in his apartment, Jake poured himself a stiff whisky and sat, deep in thought, as he idly sipped his drink, his mind filled with images of Jane the first time he'd seen her. His loins began to ache as he recalled her walking into the room. He hadn't thought a business suit could have turned him on as much as hers had. It was after all just a working outfit any career woman would wear, but to him, her suit was so sexy he'd wanted to divest her of it! As well as all the other articles of clothing she'd been wearing, until she was standing before him as naked as the day she'd been born. Then, once they were both undressed, he would make passionate love to her on top of the desk, having already sent her father packing. As the alcohol burned its way down his throat, he sighed, he had a long way to go before he would be able to fulfil any of his fantasies, which I suppose could well have been the same thoughts Jane was having about him!

Andrew arrived at Jane's flat that same evening just a little nervous at the thought of the reception he was likely to receive; deeply ashamed at his deceit in trying to set up his only daughter in marriage with a man she didn't know, brokering her marriage to an unknown man purely for his own gain. He knew he was selling her to the highest bidder but that wasn't true of course, as Jake was the only bidder! He was also ashamed at what his late wife would have said, although he knew had she still been alive none of this would have happened.

Jane answered the door to his tentative knock. By the aroma coming from her kitchenette, he knew he would be offered a meal, if not her forgiveness. She kissed him lightly on the cheek, in a distracted sort of way; giving him the impression her mind was a million miles away from cooking. Absentmindedly, she offered him a drink and then walked away, leaving him to help himself from the drinks tray that sat on a small table in the corner of the room. He noticed the enormous bouquet of roses and wondered whether Jake had sent them, but said nothing.

It was an easy meal, steak with a simple green salad and a potato dish she knew to be his favourite. A bottle of red wine stood open on the table, already set for two, as Jane had been sure her father would arrive, even though at the moment he wasn't quite her favourite person.

Conversation was somewhat stilted at first: whenever Andrew asked a question, Jane answered, but he could tell her mind was not really tuned into him and, once the meal had been eaten and coffee served, he took the initiative and started to talk enthusiastically about Jake's proposed plans for taking over the company, without mentioning the young man's other plans of taking her over at the same time! Suddenly, at the mention of Jake's name, Jane immediately became alert and, fixing her attention on her father she rounded on him.

'What did you think I would say, when Jake Adams had the temerity to tell me I must marry him, or he wouldn't save your business?'

Andrew looked at her, shamefacedly. 'Well, I thought he was just the sort of man who would make you happy and be a good husband,' he'd replied, rather lamely.

'So you know the sort of man I like, do you?' she'd asked, at the same time not giving him a chance to answer and tell her that he did know and, if he had his way it would be Jake. Jane knew herself she needed a man who was good at business and that was Jake's forte for sure, but he was too arrogant for her liking.

'I might tell you, father dear, this is not the "Middle Ages" and I'm old enough to choose my own husband!'

Continuing in much the same manner she ranted at her father until she was exhausted. At the same time Andrew tried hard to placate her, but, after a while, even he could see he was not going to have much success in trying to persuade her to his way of thinking that Jake was the ideal man for her. Jake, he decided would have to do his own persuading. Something Andrew had no doubt Jake, being an intelligent young man, would succeed in doing where he'd failed.

It was late by the time Andrew left to go to his club, promising he would call the next day. By this time, Jane had calmed down a little and went to bed, hoping to dream of her pirate, convinced now he really was Jake Adams. This time, her dream had him snatching her from off a burning galleon as it sailed across the high seas! Was it an omen of what her future was to be, she'd asked herself the next morning, when she woke, drenched in perspiration and longing to still be in his arms, as she'd been, when he'd snatched her up and swung her to safety, away from the flames and onto another galleon that had sailed to their rescue. She could still imagine the feel of his arms around her, a sensation that thrilled her and, for a few moments, she wondered if marriage to Jake might not be such a bad idea after all! Perhaps then, with the real man in bed with her, the dreams would stop. Surely it couldn't be too difficult to get a red-blooded man such as Jake to fall in love with her?

As for Jake, he already knew he was in love but he also knew he needed to learn more about women and the ways they liked to be romanced. He knew he needed to ask questions of someone already happily married so, out of several suitable married friends, he decided to ask Mark and Liza his closest friends for their advice, knowing they were sure to tell him how to go about properly wooing a woman!

Mark and Liza lived in domestic harmony as far as he knew and, after a quick phone call, he was asked to go round that same evening for a meal.

Later, carrying a bouquet of flowers for Liza and a bottle of good claret for Mark, he arrived on time at their house in the suburbs, where he intended to get as much information as he possibly could on the ways to woo and win the first real love of his life.

It was a pleasant enough evening, catching up with their news, with Jake making no mention of Jane when asked what was new in his life, fudging his answers once the questioning started to get too personal.

Mark had acted as butler for the evening, leaving Liza to do the cooking, thereby giving Jake his first lesson on a modern married couple's domestic set up.

It was their teamwork that impressed him the most. He decided that must be the first priority in his and Jane's relationship once they were married! Teamwork, with Jane taking the lead in domestic issues! Once the meal was finished and the table cleared, they moved into the sitting room, where Liza and Mark gravitated to the sofa, leaving Jake to sit in one of the easy chairs. Liza wrapped her legs over Mark's and settled herself into his arms, a picture of romantic bliss and contentment that brought a feeling of jealousy into Jake's heart, knowing this was exactly the sort of relationship he wanted with Jane.

Mark and Liza could see Jake wanted to ask them something, smiling at each other in amusement when he asked them how and when they'd fallen in love, part of which he knew already.

It was the old story of a boy meets girl, girl meets boy, they fall in love, and then they get married! They'd been in their mid-twenties when they'd met and got together. By then they were both sexually experienced and knew what they wanted in a partner and, within a few days of meeting they'd moved in together and since then had never been apart. They'd married a few months after their first date and, in Jake's mind he could see they would still be together when they were old. They now had three children and were not only lovers, but doting parents as well.

When Jake asked Mark how and when he'd proposed to Liza, Mark just laughed.

'Proposed? I think we proposed to each other. Liza said something like, how about I move in with her and I said how about her moving in with me?'

Jake looked a little nonplussed. 'So you didn't pursue her with flowers and perfume, then?

Liza quickly answered that question. 'Well, he did, but not until the ring was on my finger!'

'What do you mean by that?' Jake asked, keen to get to the bottom of the mystery called love.

'Well, sometimes men think like hunters. All the romance for them is in the chase and then, once they've caught their prey that's the end of it, no need for romance anymore, but that isn't how a modern woman's mind works. Any sensible man these days, especially one who's been brought up properly, will know that to keep a marriage alive and well, the romancing has to continue, in fact it has to go on forever! And of course, women like to be told often by their man that he loves them!'

Jake was beginning to understand. There was much more to falling in love than he'd thought. He needed to do as Liza and Mark were doing, hold hands at every opportunity, gently caressing each other as couples do when they are in love. Jake had even noticed the way Mark would put his hands affectionately around Liza's waist, gently handling her curvaceous bottom at every opportunity. Jake made a mental note to do this with Jane, once they were married! He also made up his mind he had to be like his friend at all times, whispering words of love to Jane, just as Mark did to his beloved.

Jake tried out his newfound theory on how to romance Jane several times over during the next couple of days; bombarding her with more flowers, as well as gift-wrapped parcels of exquisite handmade chocolates and the finest French perfume, all guaranteed to delight any woman, or so the lady in the store informed him as she wondered who the lucky lady was that was going to receive them.

As each gift arrived, Jane began to feel far from delighted! In fact, she had a bit of a mini panic! She didn't possess enough vases for the flowers and the perfume from them was giving her a headache! Also, her flat was too small to be overtaken by what appeared to be the entire contents of a florist's shop. The chocolates looked delicious, but if she were to keep her figure as slim as she liked they would have to go somewhere else; of course the staff at the office enjoyed them, wolfing them down and then asking when she would be having some more! As for the bottles of perfume! Do you really think she would have refused them? Certainly not! She placed the fancy bottles in a drawer of her dressing table. She might be holding Jake Adams at arm's length, but even she wasn't so stupid as to send back something that was so expensive and gorgeous, promising herself she would think of Jake, every time she used them.

Jake phoned her the evening following his visit to Mark and Liza, after Jane had decided to have an early night and catch up with her sleep. (Her sleep pattern had deteriorated somewhat ever since she'd started to dream of him) but now she'd started to dream of him in different guises; last night he'd appeared as a knight in shining armour riding on a white horse to save her from some calamity or other that even Jane thought was all rather hackneyed! Her dreams were becoming more ludicrous as the nights went by: she was always being rescued from somewhere dangerous, usually ending up with her being flung onto a canopied bed or something similar, where her rescuer would join her and where they would make passionate love until she slept, out of sheer exhaustion. She would wake in the morning with her bed sheets wrapped around her in such a way she couldn't move and with her whole mind and body clamouring for more, wishing her dreams would never end.

Jane picked up the phone and heard his voice.

'It's me, Jake. Can I come up and see you?'

Jane waited a moment. First of all, because she'd been thinking of him and secondly, because she couldn't trust her voice not to splutter as she answered. He waited. Eventually, she spoke.

'I was just going to bed, but if you promise not to stay too long I guess that would be all right. Where are you?'

Not the most encouraging words Jake had expected to hear. 'I'm downstairs. Look out of your window and you'll see my car!'

Jane walked across the room and drew back the curtains to look down at the street and, sure enough, parked under a streetlight was his Porsche, with him standing beside it, mobile phone in hand. He saw her and waved; within (what seemed like only seconds) he was knocking on her door. As she opened it she saw a look of contrition on his face.

'Come in,' she said, wishing she wasn't wearing her oldest and most comfortable dressing gown, but something a lot more glamorous. To her chagrin, Jake didn't seem to appear to notice what she was wearing. He was too busy looking at the antiques and pictures that lined every inch of the walls. His eye caught by one painting in particular that showed a woman with a small girl.

Finally, he looked at Jane. With her face was free of makeup, he could see the freckles she normally covered and then he noticed her hair had been brushed to a wonderful sheen. As his eyes travelled over her he took in the soft pale blue woollen dressing gown that hid her curves and, from where he stood he could smell the clean scent of her. He knew if he could get closer and kiss her, he would taste the toothpaste she'd used. He wanted her, knowing she was more than just his fantasy!

With a sudden flourish, he produced a bottle of champagne from behind his back and presented it to her: for a moment as she held the bottle in her hand, Jake had a sudden feeling she might well smash it over his head, fortunately for Jake, the same thought had crossed Jane's mind and then she'd thought better of it. It would, she thought, be a sinful waste of an expensive bottle of bubbly!

Leaving Jake to look some more round her sitting room, she went into the kitchen and placed the bottle in the fridge. There was no way she was opening champagne at this time of night, she would save it for another occasion. Jake thought she'd gone to get glasses, but sadly not, as she returned empty handed.

Jake meanwhile couldn't take his eyes off the painting he'd first spotted. As Jane walked across the room to join him, standing closer than he could bear, he asked her who the people in the painting were. Out of all the paintings she'd inherited from her mother, this particular one held a special place in Jane's heart, it showed her, as a young girl, standing with her mother in the garden of the family home, along with the well-loved family dog that had since died. Little did Jane know this one painting evoked painful memories for Jake of his past! It showed a bucolic scene he envied, a scene of family life he'd always wanted to be a part of; suddenly the picture filled his heart with an emotion he couldn't describe. Perhaps it was the look on Jane's mother's face that showed the love she had for her child and, unknowingly, this one painting had taken Jake one-step nearer to finding the key to winning Jane's heart.

After a few minutes, he could see how tired she was, not that she was any the less beautiful for all that. He wanted to take her into his arms and kiss her leaving her mind and body demanding more, but for the first time he'd started to understand her body language and knew it wasn't going to happen that night!

Jane tried hard to stop her yawns but, after pouring him a soft drink, he said he preferred as he was driving, they made small talk for a little while, or at least Jake did most of the talking, asking about her job, what she did etc., with Jane answering by giving him as little information as possible, playing down her senior role in the company. Her own mind racing with the million questions she wanted to ask him, but knew it wasn't the time of day to get too deeply involved: she had to go to bed and think about just one question; how was she going to avoid marrying him when she felt her heart lurch whenever she looked at him?

After she'd thanked him again for his gifts, and stifled several yawns, Jake took the hint and rose to leave, and then came his dilemma. Did he shake hands with her, or do as his inclination wanted and kiss her on her lips, leaving her breathless and wanting more? Or, did he chastely kiss her cheek, open the door and leave with his body aching with his desire.

It was the chaste kiss that won and, with his mind in turmoil Jake left, wondering what next he should do to win her for his bride?

Chapter Five

The following morning, with no appointments that day that would take her out of the office and with her paperwork up to date, Jane was talking quietly to Jessie, doing what she called "mental spring cleaning". This involved the two of them discussing what had happened work-wise over the past few weeks, especially Jane's work in America and then, the problems facing her father. Jane then told Jessie Jake Adams was involved in saving the company: prudently omitting to tell her he'd asked her to marry him after telling her father if she didn't agree to his proposal he wouldn't help at all! Neither did she tell Jessie she thought she was falling in love with him!

Jessie had listened with interest to Jane's tales of woe, regarding her father's misfortune, but with no idea as to what to suggest when the door of the main office suddenly opened and in walked Andrew.

He'd spent the previous day in the city on business, before attending a formal dinner in the evening, sleeping at his club as was usual when he was in the city. To his surprise, early that morning he'd had a phone call from Jake, demanding Andrew should talk to Jane immediately, telling her she *must* marry him!

Andrew had been shocked at the urgency and the forcefulness of Jake's conversation, as well as surprised as he'd since thought Jake might have had a re-think on his "she marries me or else" stance of the other day, but apparently not! Andrew knew only too well what Jake's answer would be if Jane didn't accept his proposal. He would withdraw his offer of help, with the outcome being the company would fold. He knew then he would be forced into personal bankruptcy as he'd put his house up as collateral against an overdraft, just to keep them going until a final solution could been found.

Andrew felt as though his world was gradually collapsing around him and he was starting to get desperate. It had even got to the stage when he was prepared to coerce Jane into a marriage she'd declared she didn't want to be a part of and, not the first time, Andrew wondered if she would ever forgive him.

With Jake's unsaid threat troubling him, Andrew had taken a chance on Jane being in her office and had called to see her, mainly to plead Jake's case, as well as his own. She must marry Jake, he decided, or all would definitely be lost.

'Not interrupting anything important, am I?' he'd asked, innocently enough, as he'd opened Jane's office door and walked in.

'Not at the moment,' she'd said, smiling at him. 'Jessie and I were just talking things over.'

Andrew laughed. 'It's always good to talk problems over with a friend,' he'd said, looking from one young woman to the other, reflecting on how his late wife had also been his greatest friend and confidante and now, apart from Jane, he had no one he could turn to or confide in.

'Perhaps you could spend some time with me this morning, Jane, if you've nothing important to do here? I need to talk to you and a walk in the park might do us both good?'

Jane wasn't so sure she should leave the office but Jessie stepped in, assuring her she would manage and with just a small amount of persuasion, Jane left with her father, with Jessie watching from a window, as they walked towards the park, wishing Andrew had come to take her out instead. She liked him. He'd always been charming to her whenever he'd come to the office in the past. She knew from Jane that since his wife had died his life had been lonely, and she knew exactly how that felt: heading for her forties and, being alone wasn't exactly what she'd wanted either and Andrew seemed to be a "lost soul", a man who needed help. *Perhaps they should get together*, she thought, *and make each other happy but then; perhaps he would want someone more glamorous?*

Jessie wasn't on Andrew's mind at that moment; he had something more important than his own love life to think about. He needed to talk to Jane. But, first of all, there was her attitude towards Jake and her answer to his proposal. Was it to be yes, or a definite no and, if the latter, what was he to do if he lost everything? Andrew knew he was going to use emotional blackmail, but when needs must, one has to resort to anything that will solve the problem and his problem right now was, that he had a workforce of men who needed to work; to earn the money to put food into their children's mouths and clothes on their backs. What stronger motive did he need than that, to persuade his daughter to do something that at the moment she was baulking at? For goodness sake he thought, exasperated, Jake Adams wasn't an ogre, he was a good man, a little inclined to be slow on the uptake when it came to women, but Andrew was sure if he married Jane she would soon get him into shape and make him into a good husband! He certainly had the potential!

On the way to the park, they stopped off at a coffee shop and bought two coffees to take with them. This park might have been smaller than most others in the area but it was beautifully kept and one of Jane's favourite places to sit and chill out during her lunch breaks from the office.

Andrew headed for an empty bench, where they sat and drank their coffees in silence, until he looked at his watch and knew he had to get a move on. Time was running out and he had a train to catch and very little time left in which to persuade her to marry Jake. He was just thinking of how to approach her when she beat him to it, pre-empting his thoughts.

'Jake Adams came to visit me last night!'

'Did he ask you to marry him?' Andrew asked, watching her face for any clue as to what she was thinking.

'No, he didn't.' Jane said sharply in reply, 'and if he had, I would have definitely have told him the answer was NO!'

Andrew didn't know what to say for a moment.

'I know you need his money, but I don't. I can look after myself, thank you.'

Andrew knew he had to say his piece and, clearing his throat and looking down at his empty coffee container, as though it was the most intriguing article he'd ever seen, he started to speak. 'You would be doing me a great favour if you did agree to marry him. It needn't be forever, just until the business is on a sound footing again and then, I promise you, if you are desperately unhappy with Jake I will help you to get a divorce!'

Jane looked at her father, her green eyes wide open in astonishment at his words but, more than that, at his suggestion he would help her to get a divorce at a later date, which surprised her even more. Well, she thought to herself that was one solution she hadn't thought of. Divorce hadn't even crossed her mind. She thought for a few moments, but it didn't seem right somehow. She knew her mother would never have approved of such a thing. Marrying for wealth wasn't something Jane had been brought up to think about, let alone do, even if it meant her father's workforce would keep their jobs. It would certainly solve her father's problems but there was more to it than that, there was her own self-respect to be considered.

'Did Jake ask you to speak to me?' She asked quietly, looking directly at him.

'Well...yes, he did.' Andrew admitted as he looked at her. He could see from her expression she was battling with her emotions. Her mouth was set in a grim line and her beautiful eyes were glittering with the unshed tears she was trying hard to suppress.

'And...?' Jane said, looking directly at him. Waiting for him to answer.

'And what?' Andrew said, shrugging his shoulders. He knew it was stalemate. He was stalling for time, but he had to get her to agree to marry Jake and then, once they were married, he would worry about her future.

But if he was the good judge of character Andrew thought himself to be, there would be no divorce, or Jake wasn't the man he'd given him credit for being! It would be up to him to keep her happy once they were married, no one could tell him what to do. Keeping a wife happy was something Jake had to learn for himself!

Making one last desperate attempt at persuading her, Andrew took hold of her hands and, looking at her with such a look of pleading in his eyes that Jane's heart ached, he said, "darling, please marry Jake, for my sake!"

Jane continued to ignore him, sitting in silence, her mind spinning and, not for the first time, she asked herself the one question she didn't really want to answer; should she marry Jake because her father desperately wanted to save his company? Should that be reason enough for her to take a chance on Jake and go through with what she knew to be an arranged marriage, just to help her father?

She thought back to Jake's proposal, to when he'd said he wanted a "proper" marriage. Did that mean having children with him as well? Could she go through with an arranged marriage, just to save her father from financial ruin? She also knew she would just be another sexual conquest to Jake, one amongst the many he'd probably had in the past?

'I'll have to think some more about what I'm going to do,' was all she could say at the moment. Her head ached, and she needed to go back to her office and think.

'Please don't say no,' was her father's quietly restrained comment. 'Jake's a nice young man, I'm sure he'll make you happy and be a fine husband, if you give him a chance, and as an afterthought, and time!'

'Oh, so you think he'll make me happy, do you?' Jane said, angry now and near to tears.

'By demanding I give up my independence and marry him without him being in love with me, or me being in love with him, just so your business can survive? But will I survive?'

Andrew knew at that moment Jane would agree to marry Jake. He just had to give her time. She was a loving young woman who cared for others and it wasn't in her nature to see men put out of work, just because she might, or might not, be in love with the man destined to save the company that employed them; a company that would soon to be forced into bankruptcy! It was obvious she understood the consequences if she refused?

The only thing he could do now was to tell Jake to be patient! To give her the time she needed to give up her independence. But Andrew knew that wouldn't be the answer Jake wanted to hear.

Father and daughter walked back to Jane's office, where Andrew noticed Jessie, in an appreciative way for the first time as a woman in her own right, and not just as Jane's assistant or friend. He'd always thought Jessie to be an attractive young woman, but today there was something more about her that caught his interest. He remembered Jane telling him of Jessie's relationship break up a few months ago. He also knew she was older than Jane, probably in her late thirties, just the right age for him. Suddenly, Andrew had the thought that as the two of them were both lonely, perhaps the next time he came into the city they could enjoy each other's company. He would make a point of asking her to go out with him, perhaps for a meal, or maybe even the theatre?

As he said goodbye to Jane, he smiled at Jessie, who felt her colour rising. She liked Andrew. He looked like a nice man, perhaps the next time he was in London she might get to meet him again. Maybe she should drop a hint to Jane, but looking across at her friend and seeing the expression on her face, she could see now wasn't the right time!

With a kiss for Jane and a last lingering look at Jessie, Andrew made his way home, where he was to wait for either for a call from Jane telling him her answer was yes, or one from Jake, calling off the deal!

It wasn't until she went back to her flat after work that Jane phoned her father, with her decision: she would marry Jake and he could phone Jake and tell him.

To her surprise, there was no phone call from Jake that evening, or even the next day, even though her father had told her he'd passed her answer on to Jake. She began to think maybe Jake had undergone a change of heart and was no longer interested in her, or in saving her father's business! But of course, no such thought had entered Jake's head at all.

It was the next evening, while she was listening to music and relaxing after a tiring day at work, that there came a knock on her door. Wondering just who it could be, she looked through the spy-hole on her door where, to her surprise, she could see it was Jake, looking devilishly handsome and patiently waiting. Jane's heart gave a quick lurch as she opened the door and in he walked, his amber eyes piercing right into hers.

'I'm so glad you decided to be sensible.' He said, going straight to the point. 'Marrying me will solve all your father's problems and, as soon as we're married, you can be sure he will be worry free!'

Without giving her time to make any comment, he continued, 'I suggest we get married by special licence within a couple of weeks…'

'Hold it. Hold it!' Jane broke in, her voice tremulous and with an edge to it that stopped Jake immediately midstream, making him take a step backwards to look at her, his eyes flashing their amber lights at her, defying her to fight him. 'I thought you told your father you *would* marry me?' He said, quietly.

'Well, yes, I did. But I didn't think it would have to be quite so soon!'

'I think the sooner the better! Especially as far as your father's business is concerned.'

Jake could see she was fighting her emotions for her eyes had filled with tears that threatened to fall at any moment: for a few seconds, Jake felt ashamed of himself. What he really wanted was to put his arms around her, hold her close and tell her everything was going to be all right and kiss her, but her defiance was off-putting. Suddenly, he realised just how much of a super-human effort it must have taken on her part to agree to marry him, considering she wasn't in love with him.

Mark and Liza had told him surprise tokens of love always went down well and, heeding their advice, he'd given much thought over the past couple of days as to what he could give her that would prove his love for her.

He put his hand in his pocket and took out a small leather covered box and held it out to her. 'I thought you might like to wear this?' he said, opening the box with a flamboyant flourish as he showed her its contents.

Jane looked at the ring nestling on its bed of midnight blue velvet. It was the most beautiful engagement ring she'd ever seen. A square cut solitaire diamond, set in platinum, encircled by a platinum band. She was speechless. She certainly hadn't expected an engagement ring and especially one she could tell must have cost a small fortune.

Watching her expression, Jake took the ring out of the box and placed it on her finger, holding her hand out to let them both admire it, for it to catch the light, where it sparkled and flashed. He bent down to kiss her, this time making no mistake and going straight for her mouth, planting a kiss full on her lips. To Jake's disappointment, Jane made no attempt to kiss him back.

'Well, do you like it?' he asked her; in a plaintive tone of voice Jane chose to ignore. 'It's a token to convince you of my honourable intentions of carrying out my part of the bargain between us.'

Just that, thought Jane; disappointed the ring was, as he'd said, merely a token of the bargain they'd made and not of his love!

'Tomorrow!' he exclaimed, 'I'll organise the licence and let you know where and when we are to be married.'

Obviously he was giving her no say at all in the matter, or manner of her wedding, an event she'd mentally had planned since she'd been a teenager, when romantic thoughts of her mythical wedding day had filled her head.

'And what am I to wear?' she asked, sarcastically, 'and who will be there?' The only two questions she could think of at that moment.

'I'm sure you have something suitable in your wardrobe, and we only need two witnesses, one of course should be your father; perhaps you could suggest a second?'

Jane's mind was racing. Why was he in such a hurry?

She took her time to give him her answer. Talk about being railroaded!

'Yes, there's my best friend Jessie, she's my assistant at work. She knows me better than I know myself! I'm sure she would like to see me getting married.' For once, Jake understood, but chose to ignore Jane's ironic comment.

Jane though would have liked to know why no one had been asked from his family, but as Jake had never mentioned having a family, she'd assumed he didn't have one. Perhaps it was a subject that upset him?

'Right then, I'll make the arrangements,' Jake said, rather brusquely 'and let you know.'

He sounded so formal, just like a door-to-door salesman who'd signed a client into a business deal and then couldn't wait to get out of her flat.

And that was how they became engaged. No words of love from either of them. It was purely a business deal as far as Jane was concerned.

Jake left without saying anything else, leaving Jane somewhat bemused and stunned by the events of the past few minutes, knowing she'd just become engaged and was planning to marry to a man she barely knew!

Jake's fortes, except when business was being discussed. So far it seemed as though it was only Jane that bore the brunt of his crass behaviour, something she hoped wouldn't continue when they were married!

Being the efficient personal assistant she was, Jessie knew straightaway the call had upset Jane but being the caring friend she was, she couldn't just sit back and not question what was wrong. Jane was still holding the dead phone in her hand, with an expression on her face that said more than a thousand words when Jessie walked in. She looked as though she wanted to strangle whomever she'd been talking to as the phone cord was wrapped menacingly around her hand. Jessie knew from the switchboard in the outer office the call had been terminated a few minutes earlier and, as she neared Jane's desk she asked, 'what's the matter, love?' Her voice was full of concern for her friend.

'I'm going to be married next Monday at 11.30 a.m. precisely, that's the matter! And I need you to be my maid of honour and a witness, along with my father, who is not just giving me away, he's selling me!'

Jessie was stunned! 'You're getting married? For heaven's sake, who to?'

'To Jake Adams, that's who to!'

'And who,' Jessie asked, stunned at Jane's pronouncement, 'is Jake Adams?'

For a few minutes, even Jessie began to wonder if Jane was having a mental breakdown. She'd certainly never heard the name mentioned before and surely, if Jane was getting married she must have fallen in love with the man, and would have told her before now? Wouldn't she? After all, they were best friends who told each other everything about any man they dated, although as far as Jessie knew, Jane hadn't dated anyone for a long time.

'It's a long story, Jessie. No that's not right, it's a short story, and it just seems to have happened a long time ago. As to where do I start? Well! Jake Adams is the man who's supposedly going to save my father's business from bankruptcy. He's the man who's going to rescue my father's company and save the jobs of all the men who work there!'

'So what's saving your father's business got to do with you marrying Jake Adams? I don't understand!'

69

'It's quite easy really. I marry Jake Adam! Jake Adams saves the business! If I don't marry him, he walks away! That's about the gist of it.

'Jake and my father have decided to broker a deal. They've come to a financial arrangement! And I'm the pot for the winner! It's going to be an arranged marriage or, put another way, I'm to have an arranged marriage for the convenience of my father!'

'You can't be serious?' said Jessie, starting to laugh but quickly smothering her laughter when she saw the look on Jane's face. She could see her dearest friend wasn't laughing at all, she was crying.

Jessie could see silent tears running down Jane's face and finally she understood. Jane was deadly serious; it wasn't a laughing matter to her at all.

'Oh, you poor darling, isn't there any way you can get out of marrying the man?' she said, at a loss to understand how Andrew Reynolds, who she'd thought to be an honourable man, and one she'd like to know better, could possibly arrange for his only daughter to marry someone she didn't know and, from the sound of it, didn't like either!

Jessie looked at her friend, a bemused expression on her face as at last Jane stopped crying, wiping her eyes, looking to be in a trance, no doubt thinking of the man she was due to marry in a few days' time, and the vows she would make she doubted being able to keep.

'So, tell me, what is this Jake Adams like? Do I know him?' Jessie asked, carrying on with her questioning, wanting to know how Jane had managed to get tangled up in such a bizarre situation at her age. It wasn't as though she was a teenager, she was an adult, a naïve one perhaps, especially as far as men were concerned, even though Jessie knew her friend had had relationships in the past, by the sound of it she had no more sense now than when she'd been ten years younger! *Ah, well*, Jessie thought, *she was in much the same boat herself, still unmarried at thirty-eight, and with no eligible man in sight!*

Jane looked at her friend. 'Jake's tall, dark and handsome, exactly what every woman wants in a man and, I also believe he's very rich as well!' This last comment she'd said cynically.

At Jane's description of Jake, Jessie shook her head. 'Rich, tall, dark and handsome men don't necessarily make the best husbands, you know?'

Jane ignored her, and her comment. 'Jake, supposedly, uses his money to help others, so maybe he's isn't as rich as all that!'

'Money isn't everything either.' Jessie said. 'Maybe it would be better if he was poor and you wanted to marry him because you loved him?'

'And he loved me? Is that what you're trying to say? It's the love part that worries me. Why does he want to marry me when he doesn't even know me?'

Jane looked hard at Jessie, 'what do *you* think I should do?'

Jessie didn't know what to say, it was a conundrum she couldn't give an answer to, except that, to her mind, any man who didn't want to marry Jane must be mad, she was the most gorgeous woman she'd ever met, stunningly beautiful with the added bonus of having an attractive personality. Jessie could well understand why Jake Adams wanted to marry Jane. Perhaps it had been love at first sight for him? It was a pity Jane hadn't fallen in love with him at the same time, then there wouldn't be a problem at all.

'Another question for you to answer for me, Jessie, is how do you know when it's love you feel and not just lust?'

Jessie couldn't give that question a straight answer either, for she was no expert on lust or love, or the intricacies of relationships, or even how you could tell whether a man loved you or merely lusted after you. She'd once thought she'd been in love with a man who she believed loved her in return, and look what had happened there? He'd met a younger woman and gone off with her in a flash! Suddenly Jessie stopped and thought of how she felt about Andrew. Whatever would Jane say if she confessed her feelings towards her father?

Meanwhile, Jane was still verbalising her thoughts about Jake Adams. 'I don't know him at all, except he's very glamorous. What is it he sees in me that makes him so adamant he wants me as his wife? Oh, yes…' she began pacing round the office, 'another thing, what if I become pregnant and he doesn't want children? He hasn't indicated he's into being a family man.'

'Are you going to turn up on Monday then?' Jessie asked, when they'd calmed down a little.

'Yes.' Jane said. 'I've decided I'm going to marry him. I'll get my revenge afterwards!'

Jessie didn't believe for a single moment Jane was serious; it wasn't in her nature to be vindictive. She wanted to ask what form her friend's revenge would take, but it was too late, as Jane had already picked up her handbag with every intention of leaving the office and, after giving Jessie one of her lovely smiles, she was out of the door and walking down the road to the tube station, deep in thought.

Chapter Seven

Andrew rang later to tell her the arrangements Jake had made for the wedding. When Jane casually asked where Jake intended to take her afterwards, Andrew knew Jake needed to get his act together as he'd made no mention of a honeymoon, or as to where they would live! Andrew of course, had forgotten to ask and, like Jane, had no idea where that would be either.

The next morning, before she went shopping for her bridal outfit, Jane phoned Jessie and told her she would be taking a couple of days off work, as she had too much to do, suggesting she join her later to pick out an outfit for her to wear as her maid of honour.

Deciding what to wear was her biggest problem. She didn't want anything long, white, or frilly, and definitely nothing that looked virginal, just a simple dress that would look special, without being too dressy. Luckily she found the perfect outfit in the designer section in the department store near to where she lived.

The dress, with a matching bolero jacket, fitted like a dream and could have been designed with her in mind. It was made of ivory shantung silk, with a fitted bodice nipped into her tiny waist and a straight skirt that had a small kick pleat at the back, and ended just below her knees. The material shimmered as she turned and twirled in front of the dressing room mirrors, the perfect colour for her burnished mahogany hair and the natural pallor of her skin.

She looked beautiful and sexy, yet at the same time demure and virginal (which she wasn't) and all she needed to finish the outfit was a headdress. For this, she chose a simple headband covered in ivory silk that exactly matched the dress and was decorated with handmade silk roses.

Finally, a pair of shoes in ivory silk, decorated with gold beads and seed pearls provided the finishing touch. As far as Jane was concerned, Jake was certainly going to get a bride who looked truly beautiful, one definitely worth every penny of the many thousands of pounds he was spending to save her father's company.

Looking good was going to be Jane's armour. She wanted to feel like every other bride on her special day, even if it was a marriage of convenience. Looking good would certainly help her to cope with what she assumed would be the most stressful and emotional day of her life.

But what about flowers? It was usual for the groom to provide them! As she looked in the mirror her only wish was, that she'd been a conventional bride, making her own decisions, but this was one wedding where the groom-to-be had taken on that mantle.

Jake, meanwhile, was just as busy in his own way, making plans for what to him was also going to be a special day in his life. He'd never envisaged getting married, let alone planning one and then, of course there was the honeymoon he'd nearly forgotten to organise.

The Dorchester Hotel had been booked for the wedding reception by Jake, as well as a suite for the first night of them being married where he intended in every sense to make Jane his wife.

It was going to be a small affair, for only a handful of people, until Andrew had convinced Jake they should invite a few more, rather than just the two Jake had at first wanted.

As for where they would live as a married couple, he'd even given that some thought as well, thinking Jane might prefer to live in her flat, small as it was, rather than in his spartanly furnished bachelor apartment in Chelsea, at least until they could get a house in the country.

Jake fully intended their marriage to be a partnership, even if Jane viewed it as a marriage of convenience and, as far as he was concerned, it was for keeps, and any decisions regarding their future life together would be made jointly. All he had to do was to tell Jane of his decision and convince her he loved her for herself, and not because he wanted to get his hands on her father's business, and for her to know he'd wanted to marry her from his first sight of her when he'd been hit by a thunderbolt of love! He might in the past been sexually aroused and satisfied by other women, but he'd never been emotionally satisfied. He certainly didn't understand the opposite sex, and even less their emotional needs, because he didn't understand his own: not telling Jane he had a mother, father and two stepparents, as well as two siblings, was the result of his emotional ignorance, an omission that was going to contribute to his downfall, but that's for later. It was too late now for him to contemplate making alterations to his plans, even knowing he'd made a fundamental error in blackmailing Andrew into persuading Jane to marry him. This worried him a little: ashamed at his lack of ethics, but his desire to possess Jane was so great he'd chosen to ignore his conscience that had started to urge him to take the conventional route of wooing and courting her before they married. There was no doubt about it; Jake Adams was going to be hoisted by his own petard! If only he'd known, he would have to pay a high price for his inexperience in the future? But, being the man he was, he managed to shrug off his doubts, thankful that Andrew Reynolds needed his help so badly he'd willingly persuaded Jane to accept his proposal and that, for the time being, was quite enough for Jake!

The wedding was destined to take place in a dull and uninspiring room, in an unpretentious registry office, housed in an old council building, not far from where Jane lived. The registrar and her assistants had tried their best to make the room as attractive as possible with the inclusion of vases full of seasonal flowers. The wedding room, as far as Jane was concerned, just wasn't the same as the old and beautiful church in the village where she'd grown up, and where she'd always imagined in her dreams of making her vows to a man she loved. This Spartan wedding would have no choir singing as her father walked her up the aisle, or bridesmaids and pageboys walking behind her. Neither would there be any of her old aunts and uncles, or all her old friends from school.

Without telling Jane, Jake had done as Andrew had suggested and invited her friend, Sylvie, but not Leo, as he was again working in America. Jake had even asked Mark and Liza, his friends to join them, but there had been no invites to his family. And then of course, there was Jessie, who was to be Jane's matron of honour and a witness, along with Andrew.

Much to Andrew's surprise, Jake was taking his role as wedding planner quite seriously: he'd even organised the flowers, a small bouquet of yellow tea roses for Jane and a smaller bouquet of spring flowers for Jessie, as well as buttonholes for himself and Andrew.

With everything in place, Jake was quite pleased with his efforts; all he could hope for was that Jane would arrive at the stated time and would take him for her lawful wedded husband and that she would do so with love, if not in her heart then at least in her mind as a possibility for the future!

Jane, she spent her last day as a single woman tidying and cleaning her flat, until the evening, when she relaxed in a bubble bath and where she lay thinking of how she would get through the next day and, more importantly, her wedding night, when she would be expected to become Jake's wife in more than name.

There had been neither sight, or sound from Jake, but her father had phoned every day to let her know how the arrangements were coming along. Again, as a prospective lover and husband, Jake was uncommonly slow-witted!

The wedding flowers were due to arrive early on the morning, as was Jessie, who intended to help Jane dress and do her hair and make-up. As for Andrew, he was going to spend the night before the wedding at his club, and would be at Jane's flat in time to escort her and Jessie to the registry office, where, Jake had assured Andrew he would be waiting.

Jane slept fitfully that last night as a single woman, her fantasy dreams even more bizarre than usual. She'd started to look forward to going to bed and being transported into another world where, no matter what was happening to her in real life, she always ended up in Jake's arms in a passionate embrace. Would her dreams, she wondered, be fulfilled once they were married?

At last, her wedding morning arrived. The day her mother had always said would be the happiest of her life. But Jane was sceptical, unsure whether this day would be special, or an unmitigated disaster. In some ways she felt like a condemned woman, heading off to the gallows, her stomach full of butterflies but, once dressed in her lovely outfit, the magic started to happen and, by the time her father and Jessie arrived she felt calm and serene, quite the opposite of how she'd thought she would feel. Strangely enough, she'd become accepting of what she was about to experience. The only part that upset her was when her father became tearful as he first saw her in her wedding outfit. He'd clutched her hands and thanked her for what she was doing to help his business; it was at this point she began to feel sick with nerves; not to the point where she was sick, but to where she could feel an inner excitement building up and, with her diamond engagement ring transferred to her right hand, she suddenly had a feeling of bravado in her heart and that's how she continued to feel, right up until she left for the registry office, where she would soon become Mrs Jake Adams!

Jake was already waiting at the main entrance door when Jane arrived with Andrew and Jessie. To her surprise, she saw Sylvie waiting as well, along with another couple she didn't recognise, but whom Jake introduced later as his good friends, Mark and Liza.

Jake's first thought as Jane alighted from the car and walked towards him was how beautiful she looked, and how lucky he was to have ensnared her, given her feisty nature. His pride in her was enormous, especially as she'd turned up, not realising how independent she was, or that, once she'd made a promise, she kept it.

Jane looked at Jake, giving him a quick once over, noting how handsome he looked wearing a lightweight Italian suit, in pale grey, that flattered his dark colouring. He'd chosen a blue shirt, patterned in soft shades of pale blue with a matching silk tie and, as they stood together on the steps of the old building, Mark videoed the occasion. To him, they appeared to be a well-matched couple about to embark on the journey of a lifetime together, but both bride and groom had their own thoughts as to the route their journey would take, surprising them, had they known they were the same!

Like everything else about her wedding, Jane had little or no say in the choice of her wedding ring either. Strangely enough, this didn't irk her at all as Jake had already demonstrated his good taste in jewellery so, when Jane saw the exquisite diamond studded platinum ring he'd chosen for her, for the first time as he placed it on her finger she was delighted.

The ceremony itself was short and simple. There were no choir boys singing hymns, no old aunts and uncles wiping tears from their eyes, and no vicar to bless them after they'd said their vows in front of the altar in the old church, but, for all that, Jane felt as though she'd taken part in a meaningful ceremony, one, much to her surprise equally as solemn. The one moment that pleased her, the most, was when Jake took the wedding ring from out of his pocket and placed it on her finger. She would remember that moment forever. He'd made his vows, his eyes never once leaving hers and, as soon as he'd placed the ring on her finger, he'd gallantly raised her hand to his lips and kissed it, bringing tears, not only to her eyes, but also to those watching in the seats behind them.

Mark recorded every detail of the ceremony, and then afterwards on the registry office steps, as they all gathered outside in the sunshine, before the bride and groom sped off to the Dorchester for their wedding breakfast.

The ride to the hotel gave them a chance to relax after what had been quite a stressful experience, both having carried out their parts with dignity. And now, sitting together in the limousine they both felt different. Jake of course was extremely happy because he'd just married the most beautiful woman in the world, one he loved with all his heart. As for Jane, she felt different too, but why should a simple ceremony have had such an impact on her senses in particular? She couldn't understand why she should feel as she did. They might have kissed, after their rings had been exchanged, but it hadn't been a proper kiss and that was how she continued to feel over the next few hours as they went through the motions of hosting their wedding reception.

The food was delicious, smoked salmon, roast spring lamb, a fruit sorbet to die for and then, of course champagne that had flowed nonstop, and then the cake, Jake had ordered especially, which they'd cut with due ceremony, after which came the impromptu speeches, made by Jake's friend Mark, and then Andrew, who welcomed Jake as his son-in-law, deliberately not making any reference to the speed of the marriage, or to Jake's part in the survival of his company, or more to the point the fact that the marriage had been one of convenience.

Jake took every opportunity during the feast to have his hands around Jane's waist, pulling her into close contact with his body. He could also be seen holding her hand, much to the amusement of Andrew and Jessie, who knew the true story, and then, when Jake raised his glass to toast Jane, and their future together, Jane had simply raised her glass and looked long and hard into his amber eyes, silently echoing his thoughts, an enigmatic smile on her lips that promised nothing.

Unbeknown to the newly-weds, Andrew and Jessie were also hitting it off quite nicely as well.

The wedding party was just about to break up when, to much laughter, Jake told everyone he and Jane had plans for the evening that didn't include anyone else. It was at this point Andrew had whispered into Jessie's ear that if she were free, perhaps she would care to join him that evening!

Of course, Sylvie, Mark and Liza had to get back to their respective homes and their children and, with everyone's best wishes ringing in their ears, the newlyweds said their goodbyes and retired to their suite in the hotel to begin their married life, away from prying eyes.

Chapter Eight

Holding Jane tightly by the hand, Jake walked her to the lift and, within a few minutes, they were at the suite he'd booked for their wedding night. He unlocked the door and pushed it open. Turning, he effortlessly picked her up in his arms and immediately she was experiencing the fantasy she'd dreamt of over the past few weeks. As he carried her across the threshold she gasped, momentarily taken aback by his actions and the opulence of the suite. Carefully, he placed her down, but without releasing his hold, intent on kissing her; just as his lips were about to meet hers so she moved her head, deflecting his kiss, at the same time deftly moving out of his arms. She heard his sharp intake of breath and the next minute his hands were on her waist and, before she knew what was happening, he'd spun her round to face him. He smiled down at her as he held her close, pinning her arms to her sides with his, his warm breath fanning her face. Looking up at him, she could see the golden shards in his amber eyes glinting at her.

Determined to stamp his authority on their relationship in the only way he knew how, Jake kept her arms pinned to her side and kissed her thoroughly, which he managed only by releasing one arm and holding her head in such a position she couldn't escape. The next minute, he'd taken full command of her mouth, with his tongue probing and tasting her and, before Jane knew it, she was responding in the same manner, her pent up emotions threatening to overwhelm her.

Jake gradually relaxed his hold as she kissed him back. Moving his hands over her body he started caressing her, first her hips, shaping the swell of them and then her breasts that he gently weighed, feeling her nipples hardening at his touch. He sensed her passion was as elevated as his own, in the way she pressed her body against his, eager to feel his arousal, moving her legs apart so she could feel him better. For some time, they stood together, enjoying the intimacy of the moment, kissing, and with Jake thrusting his body against hers, their first bodily contact since they'd met.

Jake knew he'd successfully breached her defences, when she started to caress his body in return. He could feel his muscles tensing as she moved her hands over his stomach, making their way down to the bulge in his trousers, at the same time his erection was causing him some discomfort, contained as it was by clothes he wanted to remove, that he might get his body even closer to Jane's.

Well aware of Jake's sexual excitement and his arousal, pressed as it was close to her body, Jane found her own excitement mounting. Suddenly, Jake released her, but only for a moment, as he lifted her once more into his arms. This time, Jane placed her arms around his neck as he carried her into the bedroom where he placed her tenderly down onto the huge bed that dominated the sumptuous room; a room designed to entice any reluctant bride to make love. But Jane was no longer a reluctant bride, merely unsure of Jake's qualities as a husband, even if he was a good kisser!

Jake though wasn't unsure! The next minute he was kissing her and, with his arousal pushing hard against his trousers he knew in the next few minutes he would make her his own, in the full physical sense, knowing that whatever it had cost him financially to get her to marry him, it was already worth every penny just to be on this bed, looking down into his wife's emerald eyes, already love hazed as they looked into his.

It took very little effort for him to remove her bolero jacket and pull down the zip of her dress and then, with her help, he removed the rest of her clothes, managing at the same time between them to remove his own.

Quite soon, his jacket, trousers and shirt had landed in a heap on the floor, on top of her dress and underwear. It then got more interesting as Jake climbed onto the bed and straddled her, looking down at her, as she lay naked beneath him.

Jane's first sight of Jake's naked body didn't seem to embarrass her at all, in fact she was amazed not only at her own wantonness, but also at how mesmerised she was by his erection!

Jane looked up at him, her eyes beguiling him into exploring her body, daring him as she tried to outstare him. This was where Jake's sexual experience out-weighed hers. He leant back, for a moment, letting her have her fill of his body, before smoothing his hands over hers. He began exploring every nook and cranny until any thought of revenge vanished from Jane's mind. She'd feasted her eyes on the beauty of his body, her eyes drawn to the impressive length of his erection and then to its silky feel, as she took it in her hand. She heard Jake's sudden intake of breath as she slowly stroked him, moving her hands instinctively, loving the feel of him.

Jake leant forward to kiss her nipples that were standing out with her excitement, feeling her shudder as a shiver ran through her body as his mouth suckled on them, before he moved down to her waist, defining it with his hands, committing her shape to his memory, until he wanted more, much more than touching, and then it came to the point where he stopped kissing her body and pulled her even closer, as near to his body as he could get, kissing her waiting mouth, exploring and tasting its honeyed sweetness, allowing her to do the same to him in return.

Jake continued to caress her, sure he would explode if he didn't enter her soon and then, with Jane's full co-operation, he did just that.

Jane felt as though she was falling into a bottomless chasm, a deep and dark abyss, until suddenly, she was soaring up to the light, as Jake made love to her and all her senses were satisfied, every fantasy and dream she'd ever had of making love with him, her pirate, were suddenly fulfilled.

Later, with Jane dozing, Jake left her side, only to open the bottle of champagne cooling in an ice bucket, and to fill the two fluted glasses by its side, which he then carried across to the bed, along with a silver dish full of luscious ripened strawberries.

Jane felt him return to the bed and opened her eyes; sated and dreamy from their lovemaking, her lustrous hair tousled as she looked at him from under her lashes, liking what she saw. She wanted to reach out and touch him, to sweep his hair away from his face so she could see him. She did reach out, placing her hand on his cheek in a loving gesture that wasn't lost on Jake at all. He took hold of her hand and kissed the palm, loving the way she looked. If Jane looked this good in the mornings, then being married to her was going to be a joy!

Exactly Jane's thoughts, as they sat together, naked, under the covers, feeding each other strawberries as they sipped champagne. For the first time, Jane realised that Jake, for all that he'd been a fabulous lover, had failed to tell her that he loved her!

He didn't know how to say those three simple words. Three little words that mean so much to a woman were left unsaid. It was this omission that was to prove the stumbling block in his relationship with his new wife.

Jane felt disappointed and let down, not at his prowess as a lover, but without those few words, their lovemaking had become just an act of sex. As she sipped her glass of champagne she wondered if that was how he felt. Was it just sex to him? Would his lust for her turn to love, given time?

Jake though had had no such thoughts. He was more than happy with his bride. As far as he was concerned arranging to marry Jane, as part of his saving Andrew's company had been his most inspired deal ever. The most successful piece of bargaining he'd ever done. And now, all he had to do was to consolidate his position as her lover and husband, which he fully intended doing, just as soon as they'd drunk the remaining champagne!

The theatre show they went to later was memorable, as was the dinner at an Italian restaurant, where from the welcome they received, it was obvious Jake was a favoured customer. The waiters were attentive and charming and, when Jake told them it was their wedding day, there was even more champagne drunk. By the time they finally returned to the Dorchester they were more than slightly intoxicated and definitely in lust!

Jane was the first to undress: jumping naked into the huge bed, this time, to Jake's delight, she took command. For someone who hadn't wanted to get married, Jane was certainly enjoying her honeymoon! As for Jake, he was unable to believe she could be so wanton, or so forward, enjoying their lovemaking: their joint passion secretly pleasing them both.

The next morning, Jane woke to find Jake already showered, dressed and pouring coffee from the breakfast trolley just delivered. Seeing Jane awake, he started dishing up the food, bacon, eggs, hot rolls, croissants, all freshly baked, making her realise how hungry she was. Jane laughed. It must be all the exercise from having sex that had given her an appetite! She made up her mind that today, she would talk over her role in their marriage and find out just exactly what it was Jake expected from her, as his wife, in return for helping her father! And, what she could expect from him, as her husband?

Her feelings for him had changed dramatically since they'd married. She'd enjoyed their lovemaking, just as Jake had. But what she wanted to know was, why had he'd been in such a hurry to marry her?

Jake was perfectly happy, and far from worried about his marriage. He had the woman he wanted in his life, what more could any man want?

Had he known the direction of Jane's thoughts, he could have saved himself a lot of heartache by being truthful, telling her how much he loved her, but Jake, being emotionally naïve, he didn't know how.

If only he'd known, it was his naivety that was going to get him into trouble and in a big way! If only!

Chapter Nine

Jane had been agreeably surprised when Jake told her they were going to Paris for their honeymoon. It was a city she knew well, and the hotel he'd chosen was perfect, small yet charming, with a romantic décor and a view from their room overlooking the Seine.

On their first evening in the city of love and romance they went to an intimate little restaurant on the left bank for dinner. It was an old-fashioned place, its atmosphere redolent with nostalgia for the past, as a musician played an accordion while they dined. Jake could see from Jane's face; he'd chosen their honeymoon destination well. (All thanks to a tip off from his new father-in-law that Paris was a city Jane loved.) But even though he was in the most romantic city in the world, with the woman he loved sitting opposite, Jake found it impossible to open his heart and say what was inside him.

It was a magical night, tailor made for lovers, with the sky full of glittering stars. The river turned to silver from the reflection of the moon as they walked slowly back to their hotel. Taking in the atmosphere, Jane asked Jake why he'd brought her to Paris.

'Because I couldn't resist it,' he'd replied, surprised at the expression on her face, 'I thought you would like Paris? It's supposed to be the most romantic city in the world! Also, I asked your father his opinion, and he said it was one of your favourite places.'

Jane didn't answer. What could she say? Her father had not only arranged her marriage, but also she'd found he'd even had a hand in arranging her honeymoon! Whatever next would he arrange? Would it be how many children she should have?

Jane felt bruised and mentally confused: knowing that when she'd married Jake she was merely adding another business acquisition to his portfolio. As far as she was concerned, she was quite sure he didn't love her. He might lust after her body, just as she lusted after his, but enjoying great sex in no way proved he loved her. She could see he desired her, he'd made that more than obvious, but to her mind that wasn't good enough, especially knowing she wanted more than sex, she wanted his love!

'I should thank you, for marrying me.' Jake said, as he placed his arms round her waist drawing her into a close embrace: looking down at her with his heart beating so loud he was surprised Jane couldn't hear it.

Jane looked up at him, a streetlamp shining on her face, her eyes wide open and expectant, and then *she* spoilt the moment.

'Why should you thank me? I was only doing what I'd been asked to do by my father!'

For a moment, Jake just looked at her, unable to comprehend her comment, his eyes showing his hurt at her remark; suddenly she felt mean and childish.

'It's true! You told my father you wouldn't help him if I refused to marry you, so I was more or less ordered to go through with it. I had to consider the workers at the factory. If the factory closed down there would be no jobs for them and I couldn't have that on my conscience now, could I? Marrying you was the only way I could see of getting out of the dilemma my father had created.'

Jake looked as though she'd hit him full in the stomach, all his breath knocked out of him by her blunt words; to add insult to injury she quietly carried on with her tirade.

'Jake, you married me in return for bankrolling the company and to get your hands on my father's business. I'm not stupid! I expected that if I married you there would be sex involved! Especially as you are a real heterosexual man and I'm a red-bloodied woman!'

Jane desperately wanted Jake to tell her he'd married her because he loved her, not because she came with the business, but because he wanted her for herself. But that didn't happen, even though he'd had been shaken by her outburst. But Jane wasn't finished yet!

'I knew you'd want to have sex with me in return for helping my father. I suppose I saw it as being a reasonable exchange. I just hope you haven't been disappointed?'

Jake looked at her, aghast at her words. He couldn't believe what he'd just heard. So, she'd willingly taken part in their lovemaking because her father had ordered her to marry him? He'd thought she'd participated because she wanted him as much as he wanted her, but apparently not! She'd given him the impression she'd enjoyed every moment as much as he had. He'd even thought she might have fallen a little in love with him, but obviously that wasn't right either! Was she now telling him she would only stay with him until the company was on a firm footing? And what then? Would she then file for a divorce! Well, that was never going to happen; he didn't intend losing her, even if she didn't love him. Somehow, he would make her change her mind and fall in love with him! But how that was going to happen he was at a loss to know. For once, his ego had taken a big tumble from which he couldn't see any way of getting over.

All he knew was that he had to convince Jane he'd fallen in love with her the first time he'd set eyes on her. But before he could tell her, she'd broken away from his embrace and was quickly walking away, making her way back to their hotel. What he didn't know, and couldn't see, were the tears streaming down her face.

As for Jane! *Why*, she thought to herself, *had she berated herself and spoken to Jake as she had? Why couldn't she just have been satisfied knowing she loved him? Did it really matter whether he loved her or not? Perhaps given time he would fall in love with her, until then, she would try to act, as any good wife would!*

Jake caught up with her and, in silence and with no physical contact, they made their way back to their hotel, each deep in their own thoughts. Jake's thoughts were that he intended to let his body do the convincing. If Jane's reaction to him the previous nights had been for real, then he did have something she wanted, or had that been just pretence as well?

Jane undressed in the small en suite bathroom, no wanton stripping and leaping into the bed for her that night. She came out wearing a demure nightdress, a sexless number Jessie had tried hard to persuade her not to buy.

Turning back the bedcover, she climbed in, pulling the covers up to her chin, making it obvious there would be no sex that night! (This is universally known as the angry arse treatment!)

Jake, meanwhile, had stripped down to his Calvin Klein's and was already sitting on the edge of the bed when Jane appeared wearing her virginal nightdress. He smiled at her as though nothing was wrong, hoping she would respond in a way that would save the situation from deteriorating any further but, from the frosty look she gave him, he knew it wasn't going to be as easy as he'd thought, trying to convince her of his true feelings. All that mattered was that he loved her and, quite frankly, he didn't give a fig for her father's business. That had just been a front to get her to marry him!

Jane ignored him, her buttoned up, high-necked attire successfully giving out its "keep out, forbidden territory" sign.

Jake got the message, but that didn't stop him wanting to rip the bloody thing off to reveal the body he'd worshipped the night before. He was unused to having a woman unwilling to sleep with him, especially as all his previous conquests had been more than willing, without him even offering marriage!

Sitting on the bed in his underwear, Jake was in a quandary as to what he should do next. But Jane already had her back to him, pretending to be asleep. But really she was waiting for him to do or say anything that would make her feel loved as his wife, and not as a piece of bargaining material, but Jake misread the situation and her signals, and therefore, he failed to respond.

For a man, intelligent enough to be successful at making millions of pounds in business deals, when it came to professing his love to the woman he'd married, Jake Adams was tongue-tied and inordinately stupid and, moreover, he was sadly lacking in the romance department.

With Jane under the bedcovers, feigning sleep, Jake knew the chances of him making love to her that night were going to be quite slim, possibly non-existent. He truly believed he wouldn't be holding her in his arms that night and therefore, the three little words he wanted so much to say, were to remain unsaid!

For several hours neither of them slept. They tossed and turned until, exhausted they finally did fall asleep, gravitating quite naturally into each other's arms and, from then on, it didn't take long before Jane's high-necked and demure virginal nightdress lay on the floor, quickly to be joined by Jake's underwear. It started with a kiss, which soon led to them caressing each other, to the point where there was no return. But even then, at the height of his passion, Jake still couldn't say what Jane wanted desperately to hear until finally, she realised if she wanted to have Jake in her life, and her bed, then she would have to forget hearing the words she'd thought to be so important and instead, concentrate more on his actions. Maybe in time he would be able to tell her he loved her, until then, she would just have to be content with having him as her husband!

With their honeymoon in Paris over, the newly-weds returned to London, to live in Jane's flat. Jake didn't care where he lived as long as it was with Jane. His apartment had merely been a place to sleep when he wasn't travelling. He'd decided it was better to rent it out but so far, they hadn't talked a great deal about their future together. It was early days as far as Jake was concerned, unlike Jane who wanted to know where she stood in their relationship. Perhaps that's a woman thing, wanting the security of knowing all the ends are neatly tied up but for Jake there was nothing to discuss. As for Jane, she intended continuing with her career, until the day came when Jake admitted he loved her and then she would think seriously about their future together, along with the possibility of them being parents!

Chapter Ten

The newlyweds spent their first weekend together collecting Jake's possessions from his Chelsea apartment, then moving Jane's belongings around to give them more room. It seemed odd to both of them to be sharing a bed with a comparative stranger, even more so for Jane, as her bedroom had once been her refuge. Getting to know her new husband was proving easier than even she had expected. Jake might not know the rudiments of courtship, or how to say the words of love Jane wanted to hear but he was easy to live with. Their sex life was good and frequent. Unable to take their hands off each other so far they'd made love in all the rooms. By the time Monday morning came round and work beckoned for them both, Jane had found her love for Jake growing. They'd even managed to establish a routine of sorts. And, from the look on his face, even Jake was finding married life to his liking, even if at first it had seemed strange for him to be living with someone else, especially a woman! He'd suddenly gone in one great leap from being a fully-fledged bachelor, to a married man with responsibilities. A difficult enough transition for most confirmed bachelors, but even more so for Jake, who hadn't lived as part of a family since he'd been sent away to his all boys boarding school at the age of eight, and then at eighteen he'd gone to university, where he'd lived in a male only hall of residence. From there, he'd gone to America on a scholarship where once again he'd lived in an all-male hostel, until finally, on his return to London, he'd moved into his own apartment in Chelsea. It was somewhat different for Jane. She'd lived at home with her parents, until she left for university and even there she'd shared a house with three other girls, before moving into her own flat when she first started work.

It must have been a week or so later, before Jane turned her attention to her father, whom she hadn't seen since her return from Paris. They'd spoken often on the phone and he'd sounded fine, which was itself an improvement as to how he'd been previously, but so far she hadn't seen him in the flesh.

Before her marriage, she'd worried constantly about him and then more so, once she knew of his financial problems. It was his health that was her biggest worry. She'd seen him looking more and more haggard as the days had passed, ageing, almost overnight, as he became a shadow of his former self. Rightly so, she'd become quite concerned, which was the main reason why she'd agreed to his outlandish request that she should marry Jake. When she did see him, a week or so later, she was completely bowled over. To her surprise his health had improved enormously. He'd changed, and for the better. She'd even remarked to Jake on how much fitter her father was looking. All due, Jake told her, to the company's finances being sorted out and the business once more on its way to being as financially successful as it had always been.

Jake knew from his past experiences of stepping in and helping companies with financial problems, just how much money worries are the killer ingredient for making anyone ill and, unfortunately, Andrew wasn't the exception. It always amazed Jake just how quickly someone's health problems could be cured merely by an injection of money. It always improved what had once been a disastrous situation, turning it into a good one! So Jane was pleasantly shocked when Andrew called into her office to see her, amazing her, when she saw him in the flesh. Even after such a short time, there'd been a tremendous transformation in his health, all due, as she thought, to her new husband!

It was as Jake had told her; an injection of money had certainly been the biggest part of Andrew's cure! He'd finely been able to relax, especially now he was no longer beset with financial worries and all thanks to his new son-in-law being a multi-millionaire. Unlike Jane, who had no care that Jake was worth millions! She knew she would have fallen in love with him even if he'd been penniless!

When she saw her father, she'd done a double take, unable to believe the transformation. First of all, he had a new zest for life, made obvious by the spring in his step and his bubbling enthusiasm for Jake and the business. And then there was his appearance, especially his hair! It had finally turned completely to silver, and had been cut in a style that made him look even more handsome and distinguished, and much younger than his years. She was so impressed by his rejuvenation she thought he should take a holiday, and said as much to Jake as they began preparing the meal Andrew was due to share with them later. Perhaps, she thought, after they'd eaten would be the ideal time to discuss with him taking some time away from the factory, now it appeared to be back on form with a new manager installed!

It was an enjoyable evening for Andrew. He'd enjoyed his meal and his conversations with his daughter and Jake, but it wasn't until he was about to leave Jane told him it was time he took a holiday and started to enjoy his life again, especially now the business was thriving.

At first Andrew had scoffed at the idea, refusing point blank to even consider taking time away from work, and then Jake had butted in, telling him he needed him to be fully fit, especially if he was to take over the running of the company again.

Andrew had listened and taken note, but had said nothing, until Jake told him, straight out that he wanted him to enjoy work, not to find it a drag and it was then Jane had her say.

'As you know, I'm entitled to cheap holidays for my immediate family. If you're worrying about the cost, it's one of the perks of my job. If you go into the office tomorrow and speak to Jessie, she'll tell you what's on offer at the moment.'

At the mention of Jessie's name Andrew started to wonder whether Jane was aware he'd taken Jessie out to dinner after the wedding and that since then, they'd started an affair! Jake was vaguely aware of this but, as yet, hadn't thought to confide his suspicions to Jane, believing his father-in-law's personal life was just that, personal, and nothing to do with them! This just goes to show that Jake wasn't savvy in his relationships with women, and neither was he thinking like a husband. As everyone knows, wives want to know everything there is to know!

With Jane pushing him to agree to her suggestion, Andrew's expression suddenly changed and he became quite enthusiastic! Agreeing he would indeed go and see Jessie the next day.

Later that evening, lying in bed next to Jessie after they'd made love, Andrew told her of Jane's plans for him to take a holiday!

It had been getting to know Jessie that had really changed his life; being paired together, and acting as witnesses at Jane and Jake's wedding. Seeing Jessie sitting alone, once Jane and Jake had left the reception to start their honeymoon and after everyone else had gone to their respective homes, had been a turning point for them both.

Andrew had asked rather tentatively, if she had to get home to someone. If not perhaps they could spend the evening together?

Jessie said she was on her own and, being more than a little attracted to him, of course she agreed was being as attracted to him, as he was to her and why not?

Jessie was an attractive young woman, who looked equally good out of her clothes, as she did in them, as Andrew found out later when, to his delight, he'd speedily removed them after she'd shown she was more than willing to go further, when it came to saying goodnight at the door of her flat. Instead of letting him just give her a chaste kiss on the cheek, she'd taken the initiative and put her arms around his neck, drawing his head down to meet her lips, which had then turned into a long, lingering and meaningful kiss.

The way she'd moulded into his body made it quite clear she didn't want him to leave, which was the way Andrew had also been feeling.

It had been some time since Jessie had held a man in her arms, or been in such close proximity to one, but she knew, from feeling Andrew's arousal pressing against her, as she leant against the door, he was feeling the same. Being bold, and taking the initiative, she took him by the hand and led the way into her bedroom, where it seemed quite natural for them to undress each other and make love.

To their mutual delight, lovemaking proved to be wonderful. They were on the same wavelength and later, as they lay together, spent and gasping for breath, they both knew they were right for each other as well. Andrew was everything Jessie had ever wanted in a man; he was kind and loving, but best of all, he was a sexual partner who'd considered her wants and needs first.

Even more than that, he made her laugh! A prerequisite, she thought, for any happy relationship. It takes a clever man to laugh a lady into bed!

As for Andrew, Jessie had all the qualities he needed. He knew he was falling in love with her, until the next morning, when he woke up with his mind was full of doubts. Was he was doing the right thing? Instead of being happy at his good fortune, he'd woken, racked with guilt. Seeing Jessie lying next to him, with her hair spread out like a golden cloud, it was as though by making love to her he'd dishonoured Isabel's memory. His guilt made all the worse because Jessie was so much like Isabel in personality! Perhaps that was the reason he'd been so drawn to her?

Jessie could see for herself Andrew was having second thoughts about being with her and, rather quickly, she realised perhaps she shouldn't build up her hopes of it happening again. Maybe it had been the dinner for two at an intimate and romantic restaurant, where they'd consumed far too much red wine responsible for them ending up in bed. Or perhaps she'd been too eager and desperate for love and was now expecting too much of him, especially as Jane had told her how her father had slipped into a deep depression after her mother's death. She could see from his face he felt guilty and, instinctively she knew this wasn't something she could cure with a witty remark and a laugh; it was more serious than that. Andrew had to deal with his guilt and his demons in his own way, especially if they were to have a future together.

Later that morning, he returned to his country home, his emotions in turmoil, torn apart by his guilt and unsure of what he should do.

He'd been devastated when Isabel had died and, for a long time, he'd grieved at his loss and was still grieving, for how can you forget someone you've loved so deeply and for so long without feeling some measure of guilt? He'd known Isabel since they'd been youngsters, both growing up in Yorkshire. They'd fallen in love in their teens, marrying when they were both twenty-one years old and, after a couple of years, they'd become parents to Jane.

The three of them had lived happy and contented lives until suddenly, Isabel had been taken from them. For a long time, his life had ceased to have any real meaning.

He'd never thought of looking for someone else to love until he found Jessie. It was the vibrancy of her personality that had first attracted him when he'd met her at Jane's office, and then, once he'd got to know her, she'd made him feel young again, and now he didn't know what to think, he was confused!

He spent some time looking through the box of photographs Jane had spent time sorting out, hoping they would eventually be included in the family albums. Andrew picked up one of his favourite photographs of Isabel and sat looking steadily at her image, until his eyes closed and he slept in his chair, waking later with his head clear and his thoughts lucid. For the first time in months, his depression had lifted; it was as though Isabel had given him her blessing to go forward with the rest of his life, and more than that, her permission for him to fall in love again.

By the time Jane had told him he should take a holiday, Andrew had well and truly fallen in love with Jessie. Now he was secretly hoping to make a possible holiday into a honeymoon! As far as he was concerned, there was no point in waiting! He wasn't a callow youth waiting to grow up; he was an adult who'd fallen in love with a wonderful woman, for the second time in his life!

But Andrew wasn't the only one with guilt feelings, so was Jessie. Not that she felt guilty for falling in love with Andrew, it was just that, so far, she hadn't said anything to Jane! She felt sick at heart for not telling her best friend she was in love, neither was she ashamed of what had happened, she was just afraid of Jane's reaction; wondering if she would object to losing her father to her friend?

Perhaps Jane would think she was too young for him? Or even that she was a "gold digger", or worse still, that she was looking for a "sugar daddy"? None of these things were true of course, as Andrew had little or no money, ever since his company had been in financial trouble, his only asset was the house in the country, and he'd used that as collateral against a loan for the business. Fortunately for Andrew, Jake had paid this off, but even so, half of the asset in the house rightly belonged to Jane, bequeathed to her in her mother's will. In any case, Jessie wasn't interested in country houses; she'd said she wasn't the country house type! In fact, she hated being in the country for more than two or three consecutive days. The fresh air, or so she claimed, gave her a headache, even going so far as to say it was too quiet for her liking; she much preferred the buzz of the city with its noise and bustle and wanted nothing more than to live where there was a vast choice of entertainment and restaurants, all available within minutes of her front door; as for shopping? How did people in the country manage, when there might only be one small shop in the village, with hardly any to stock a newcomer from the city might want? How could she live without the shops in Oxford Street being within easy reach?

Having made up her mind, years ago, living in the country wasn't for her. Jessie knew she was a city girl at heart, as for Andrew, he came to realise his life would definitely change if he chose to live with her!

Jane, and Jake, left for work at their usual time the next morning, going off in opposite directions, each looking forward to the following weekend, not knowing any plans they might have made, as well as their lives, were about to change drastically.

Jake's day had started happily enough. He'd briefly kissed Jane at the main door of her apartment, before walking to where he'd parked his car. As for Jane, she'd watched her handsome husband drive off, before striding to the underground to make the short journey to her office.

Jake had no urgent plans for the day, except to speak to his mother, who was worried about his half-sister, Sara who was at college in London and who shared a flat with two other students. At just nineteen years old, Sara was, in Jake's opinion immature for her age. She looked much older, being tall and attractive, with a model figure and, because of this, she was a big concern to his mother, especially knowing her daughter was too young and trusting; in fact, for her age she was quite naïve and gullible.

She'd been born and raised in Italy, in the small community where her mother and father lived and where they ran their hotel and holiday spa complex. Unfortunately, living in such a rural community hadn't prepared her for life in a cosmopolitan city, such as London and even Jake had been concerned when she'd insisted on sharing a house with two other girls, instead of moving in with him when she arrived in London to study. It would have been a bit of a squash in his place as he only had one large bedroom and a much smaller one he used as a study, but he could understand why she wanted to be independent; she was after all of age, and could live her life as she wanted but, for his mother's sake, Jake, had agreed to keep an eye on her.

Since meeting Andrew and being involved with his business, and then falling in love with Jane and getting married, his mind had been fully occupied with other things and, of course, as we already know, he hadn't told Jane about his family and this, he was beginning to realise, was going to be a problem before too long; a problem he would have to address; a fact that came to his mind when he finally spoke to his mother an hour later and she told him Sara had gone missing!

Once Jake had finished his call, and had assured his mother he would find her, he headed straight to the student house. Luckily he knew her flatmates quite well and they were still at home. Sara had apparently left a note, saying she was going away with a young man she'd met and fallen in love with through the Internet and wouldn't be returning. According to the girls, her relationship with this man, whose name they didn't know, had started some months ago when she'd logged on to a chat room site and had found a young man who'd said he was looking to make new friends. Being young and naïve, Sara believed him after she'd seen the photo he'd posted on the site that showed him to be young and attractive. She also believed him when he told her he had a good job in the city. Her online relationship had started quite innocently and had progressed from there, with him flattering her and persuading her to tell him more about herself than was wise, until finally, he'd wheedled himself into her affections, grooming her by telling a pack of lies.

Sara, believing his flattery and all else he'd told her to be true, she was convinced she'd fallen in love. And then, when he suggested they should go away together, and that he would look after her, she'd been foolishly bedazzled by his attention and, quite soon she was more than willing to do as he suggested.

Her friends had started to worry when she'd told them, a few days earlier, of her intention to go away with the man. They tried to persuade her not to be so foolish, saying she didn't know him and, being more savvy and streetwise than her, they even told her they didn't believe him to be the young and attractive man she imagined him to be, but Sara wouldn't listen. She was adamant; she knew what she was doing, and there was nothing more to say, she'd fallen in love and could look after herself.

Thankfully, her flatmates had the good sense to contact her mother the next day after they had read the note she'd left, realising she'd already gone to meet him, unaware later, by involving Jake, they would be putting into action a chain of events that would have a catastrophic effect on his and Jane's marriage.

Until that morning, Jake had no idea chat rooms could be so dangerous but, once he knew what had happened, he searched on Sara's computer to see if he could find any clues as to where she was likely to have gone, but without success. Thinking logically, he went through all his options and came to the conclusion she must have left by taxi; she couldn't have gone far carrying a fairly large suitcase, surmising she must be heading either to the coach, or railway station. Jake plumped for the latter, choosing the station nearest to her flat.

Thankfully, it didn't appear to have been more than an hour or so since she'd left, as the girls had heard her closing the door behind her as they were getting up.

Jumping into his car, Jake raced off to search for her, parking his car as near as he could to the station. To his horror and amazement, he saw her immediately he entered the station. She was sitting with her back to him, her luggage at her feet, a much older man sitting on the bench beside her. From the man's body language, Jake correctly surmised this must be the man she'd intended running away with.

Not wanting to cause a commotion, he quickly walked to a position where he could observe what was happening, without Sara seeing him. She looked far from happy and, even from a distance it was quite obvious this was not the attractive young man she'd been expecting to meet.

Jake thought the man to be in his late forties. He looked seedy and unkempt, even disreputable; certainly not the type of man any young woman would want in her life, let alone his young and impressionable sibling.

Jake moved his position so he could see her more clearly, making his way towards the shops that lined the concourse; keeping in the shadows, but ready to spring into action at the first signs of her leaving with the man. From her expression, Jake realised she was agonising over her dilemma. He had to fight his natural instinct to rush over and drag her away, knowing he had to let her make her own decision to leave, then, once she had, he would be at her side.

It took some time for that to happen, because the man appeared to be persistent. His head close to Sara's, obviously trying to persuade her to go with him, at the same time, Jake was silently willing her to get up and leave. Suddenly, Sara did stand up; at the same time the man grabbed her by her arm and tried to pull her back down onto the bench, but somehow, she found an inner strength and pushed him away. It was then Jake rushed over and pushed his way between them, his face contorted with rage as he told the man, in no uncertain terms, to leave his sister alone or he would call the police and have him arrested! The man didn't take telling twice, for he could see Jake meant business, and had the muscles to stop him if necessary. Without waiting for Jake to carry out his threat he promptly left, legging it out of the station, leaving Jake to deal with his distraught half-sister, who'd flung herself into his arms once she'd recognised him as her rescuer, clutching at him as she sobbed with relief.

'Oh Jake, what have I done?' She wailed.

'Nothing that can't be mended.' Was all Jake could say as he held her close, his relief at finding her safe flooding through him, thankful he'd saved her from what could have been an ugly situation? He couldn't do anything other than hold her close, not until her tears had slowed sufficiently for him to steer her out of the station, to where he'd parked his car and where they sat for some time as she tried to control her emotions. As her sobs subsided, Jake asked her how she'd managed to get herself into such a situation in the first place.

It wasn't a question Sara wanted to answer, full of despair as she was and deeply ashamed at her own stupidity, quite different from the normally confident, and outgoing young woman he'd seen growing up. But now, sitting in his car, she was full of remorse as she finally acknowledged the man had duped her, realising as well, he was probably a pervert with only ill intentions towards her.

Sara knew she'd had a lucky escape and gradually her tears lessened, until, at Jake's suggestion she should inform the police of what had happened, which had caused her to burst into tears again, only calming down when he promised her he would say nothing.

It was bad enough, she'd said, their mother had to know of her foolishness, without the whole world having to know as well.

Realising how stupid she'd been, she then told Jake she'd already written a letter to the principal of her college, informing him she wouldn't be completing her course. Jake took her in his arms, trying to console her as her tears started again.

'You're not going to do anything so foolish until you've really thought this through. You have to think of your future. You need those qualifications, so maybe you should take the principal into your confidence and let him be the one to advise you. I'll talk to him if you like, but I think you should go home for a while and get over what's happened.'

Jake even promised to talk to her flatmates, and let them know she was safe and, knowing his mother would be the best person for Sara to be with, he drove back to his apartment, as she'd refused point blank to go back to her own place. At least he would know she was safe there, until he could get her onto a plane and out of his hair.

And that was how Jake came to make yet another big mistake! Had he told Sara he was married, it might have saved the situation between him and Jane from later going into free fall! As clever as he was, Jake made an error of judgement in Jane's eyes, which would prove to be unforgivable! Also, had he known Jane had seen him kissing Sara, and then walking into his apartment with her, the same gorgeous young blonde she'd first seen him with, the evening she'd been at the hotel with Leo and her father! Had she been aware the self-same blonde was in fact Jake's half-sister, the outcome would have been quite different. Unfortunately for Jake, Jane didn't know! But, as it is said, that's life!

Jane's day, like Jake's, had started off quite nicely. She'd arrived at her office with no thought her life was about to change dramatically, until she started to read a fax from head office waiting for her on her desk.

Jessie had walked into the office later than usual that morning, looking flustered, giving Jane a look that, had Jane not been so engrossed in reading the fax she would have noticed. The fax asked that Jane go immediately to New York and take over from one of her colleagues who'd been taken ill in the middle of a training programme.

Jane was none too pleased to be going away at such short notice, especially now she was married, it wasn't something she wanted to do, but she had no choice as it was part of her job as a senior consultant to step in when needed. Jane passed the fax across to Jessie, who by now had regained her composure. She looked at Jane. 'Jake won't like you going away, will he?'

'Probably not, but he knows I have to travel sometimes with my job and, just because we're married it doesn't mean I can't do special assignments. I was rather hoping nothing would come in for a while but I'm sure he'll understand. I'll give him a call and tell him what's happened. Would you mind making a reservation for me on the earliest flight out while I clear up here?'

Jessie could see any chance of having a heart to heart conversation with Jane, where she'd intended confiding her own news, would have to wait.

Andrew had spent the previous night at Jessie's flat after his dinner with Jane and Jake. After an energetic bout of lovemaking he'd suggested to Jessie she should join him on holiday. Not only did he ask her to go on holiday with him but also, much to her surprise, he'd asked her to marry him. She'd been stunned at first, thinking it was too soon, but, without hesitating, she'd accepted, knowing he was exactly the man she'd been waiting for and, at their age, what was there to wait for? Her late arrival at work had been down to them talking until the early hours, after they'd decided to keep their plans secret for a while longer, and then oversleeping! They planned on waiting until they could tell Jane and Jake together, but Jessie did so want to drop a hint to her friend she'd got herself a new man in her life! But Jessie was going to have to be patient as; unfortunately, this wasn't going to happen for quite a while!

Leaving Jessie in charge, Jane left the office, intending to make her way home to pack, but not before she'd done some food shopping for Jake. So far, she'd had no success in contacting him; even his office didn't know where he was. She wasn't worried about leaving him to look after himself, as he'd already proved he could do that, without any help from her.

Once she'd finished shopping, Jane decided to take the bus home instead of the train, as it stopped only yards away from her flat. As she sat gazing out of the window, the bus suddenly came to a halt by road works and, for a while, her attention was taken by this activity until she realised this was the street where Jake had his apartment. As she watched the activity in the road she was suddenly shocked to see Jake getting out of his Porsche with the same beautiful girl she'd seen him with at the hotel.

Amazed at seeing him, Jane watched as he walked towards the main entrance door to his apartment, with the girl holding onto his arm in such a possessive manner it showed she was more than just a friend. He even had the temerity to bend down and kiss her! Jane's immediate reaction was one of anger. Why, she asked herself, was Jake taking the young woman into his flat? He'd said he was going to sell it? Perhaps what he really intended was for it to be a love nest for his extra marital activities? To say she was incensed with anger was an understatement. By the time she reached her flat it's fair to say Jane was incandescent with rage, and jealousy. So much for Jake's eagerness to make love to her each night, as though she was the love of his life, when obviously she wasn't!

Perhaps he had a problem? Or was he a sex addict? Perhaps that was the reason he wouldn't or couldn't say he loved her? And that when he left her to go to work each day, in reality he was bedding other women!

The first thing Jane did when she walked into the flat was to ring his mobile number; much to her annoyance it was still switched off. She then tried his office number, where his secretary told her she had no idea where Mr Adams could be found, or who he might be seeing, as she didn't have control of his diary! The only other person, who might know what Jake was up to, was her father and even he was unobtainable, which Jane thought rather strange. His secretary told her he'd been away from work that day and when Jane asked if it was because he was he ill, not that he'd shown any signs of ill-health when she'd seen him the night before, the woman assured her he was in the best of health; in fact, she even told Jane she'd never seen him looking better!

This was getting her nowhere; his club had no knowledge of him either, as he hadn't stayed there in over a month, which also seemed very odd, as where else would he have stayed when he'd visited her and Jake. She then called Jessie, who had no explanation either, as to whom Jake could possibly have taken to his flat. Perhaps, she suggested, the woman might be someone interested in buying his apartment! This Jane knew wouldn't be true from the way she'd seen him kissing the young woman! As for the whereabouts of her father, Jessie had crossed her fingers and told Jane she didn't know, as he hadn't called? This wasn't true. Andrew had called only a few minutes earlier, with no intention of speaking to Jane and neither could Jessie have repeated their conversation!

Jake wasn't used to discussing his comings and goings with anyone. He answered to no one for his actions, and so, that evening, as Jane watched the hands of the clock go round, she waited for a phone call that was never going to happen. If Jake had walked into the flat at that moment, Jane was certain she would have lost her temper, not something she normally did, but these were extenuating circumstances, and Jake would have learnt yet another lesson, in how to behave as a married man with responsibilities. Jane even debated going to his flat, then thought better of it, she didn't intend to demean herself in front of his other woman, especially if her hunch had been correct and he was having an affair.

By the time she left for the airport the next morning, Jane had heard nothing from her erstwhile husband and was devastated, believing their lovemaking had been performed by a man with no morals. And, like her marriage, their bedroom antics had just been a sham! It didn't take long for Jane to convince herself Jake had married her merely for his own financial gain after all.

By the time Jake phoned the flat it was too late, as by then, Jane was on her way to America. He was ready to leave for the airport with Sara and, thinking Jane must also be on her way to work, he'd tried her mobile number, to his annoyance that too was switched off. There was nothing he could do but wait until later, and contact her at her office.

Much as he loved his young half-sister, Jake didn't want to be saddled with her for any longer than was necessary, as far as he was concerned he'd done his duty by her, and his mother and, once Sara was on her flight home, he intended finding out where Jane had disappeared to as a matter of priority. He knew he needed to get in touch with her and give her an explanation as to where he'd spent the night and why. Unfortunately for Jake, that wasn't going to happen for some time to come.

Jake watched Sara's flight take off on time after an emotional farewell on her part, and after he'd promised to visit her and his mother before the summer ended. At last he was finally free to make his way back to the city, and to Jane's office, where he fully expected to find her.

The receptionist told him Jane had left that morning on the early flight to New York on urgent business, which explained why he couldn't get hold of her. He then asked to speak to Jessie, but she too was unavailable, taking time off for personal reasons the girl explained, adding she was sorry, but she didn't know where she'd gone!

Knowing Jane would be in contact with her office at some point in the day, Jake asked she be informed he needed to talk to her urgently, at the same time, knowing this might be a problem, as the time differences in America always messed up one's life.

It was all very disappointing for Jake, unused as he was to not getting his own way, but he was still hopeful Jane would find a way to speak to him, especially if their last night together had been anything to go by?

Jake thought back to that night, when he'd held her in his arms and, for a few moments, he wondered, if he did have a problem and, if so, how could he repair it if Jane wouldn't talk to him?

The worst idea Jake ever had was not telling Jane he had a family, or them he'd fallen in love and was going to marry the most beautiful woman in the world. It was as though his thought processes had become addled the moment he'd fallen in love, even to the extent it had affected his business dealings.

He'd used his emotions as a bargaining tool with her father, just to get her into his bed, something he would never have done before. Knowing all this, Jake decided he would have to admit his inadequacies to Jane, and to her father, even to his parents and stepparents, something he wasn't keen on doing, but it would have to be done if he was to convince Jane he loved her more than life itself.

His next decision was to drive across the city to the factory where he knew he should be able to find Andrew, but when he arrived there was no sight of him and no one knew where he could be found either! It just wasn't Jake's lucky day for sure, and neither would it be for a long time to come!

Jake became quite angry with himself, for not phoning first, and then, with the world in general, when he was told Andrew would be away for a few days and wouldn't be back until the following week; it was at this point his suspicions Andrew was having an affair with Jessie really took root in his mind.

By the time he returned home to Jane's flat, Jake was thoroughly fed up with the events of the past two days. He'd gone from being in total control of his life, as he thought, then married to a woman he loved and whom he'd begun to believe loved him in return, to suddenly having his life shifted right out of kilter. Much to his annoyance his complacency had been jolted and, as he liked nothing more than order in his life, Jake was getting increasingly frustrated; at the moment he didn't seem to have any control over it at all!

Jake knew he only wanted to be with Jane; his business interests no longer came first. He wanted his family to know and love her as he did and then it struck him, once they did know, they would have to learn they no longer had first call on his time and would have to sort out their own problems and then he stopped, as he thought of the repercussions when he told them? And what about Jane, when was he going to tell her? Certainly not in a phone call, it had to be face to face and, for that to happen, she had to be back home! He would just have to bide his time!

Later that evening, he had a call from his mother telling him Sara had arrived home safely. Listening to the background noise as she was speaking, Jake assumed she was calling from the restaurant. He thought of his mother's life now, and how different it had been from when he'd been young and his parent's had first divorced.

To make ends meet, his mother had taken a job as a kitchen helper at the local Italian restaurant near to where they lived. Because she was a brilliant cook, it was only natural when the usual cook had an accident she had stepped in to help out. She'd cooked superbly that night and had so impressed the owner he offered her a full-time job.

Many months later, she fell in love with Stefano, a young and handsome relative of the owner who'd arrived from Italy to work as the restaurant manager. Within a few months they were married.

Jake liked Stefano enormously; unfortunately, his own father didn't. He wasn't prepared for another man, and a foreigner at that, bringing up his son, so he insisted Jake should be sent away to a boarding school. Jake's mother tried all ways to prevent this, but she was told Jake had to do as his father wished and that was the end of that.

This was the one event that had so traumatised Jake, stunting his emotional growth to such an extent that over the years it had affected his relationships with women, leading Jake to blame his mother for sending him away.

From then on, Jake shared his holidays between his parents and their new partners, as by then his father had also remarried. The best holidays for Jake though, were the ones when he arrived home for the holidays and spent time in the flat with his mother, Stefano, and their baby daughter, Sara.

One day, quite unexpected, Stefano received a letter informing him he'd inherited an old and aristocratic Italian title, along with a run-down property in Tuscany from a bachelor uncle. Overnight, Stefano become an impoverished landowner and a Count and his, and Jake's mother's lives' were about to change drastically!

It was decided they should go to Tuscany and see exactly what it was that Stefano had inherited and, of course, when they saw the ramshackle building, that had once been an old manor house, along with several other old barns and out buildings, they wondered what they could do with it all?

It was a small estate, situated at the top of an old medieval village, with the most outstanding views over the countryside, in an area already popular with tourists, and that was twenty years ago. At the time, Jake's mother and Stefano couldn't believe their luck. They knew they could live there and make the old buildings into a wonderful home and a business and, as they were both talented, with lots of ideas they knew they could make it a success. That's how they came to be hoteliers and restaurateurs, in one of Italy's most beautiful regions.

At the end of that first holiday, Jake had to return to his boarding school, leaving his family to move permanently to Italy in the next month and start renovating the buildings. By the time of his next holiday, they were well on their way to having most of the buildings finished and, over the next few years the business gradually grew and prospered, as did Jake's education.

As he got older, so he spent longer spells of his holidays helping his mother and stepfather, doing everything and anything that needed to be done, never minding that most of it was hard work.

To Jake, it was like watching a dream unfold as the old buildings took on a new life. Once he'd been to America and had graduated from university, and he'd been "head hunted" Jake finally found his own niche in life.

He had a natural talent for making money! Enormous sums of it, with the added bonus, he enjoyed the buzz making it gave him!

He was also able to help his mother and Stefano out financially, as they struggled to get the renovations to some of the old barns finished, as they expanded their venture. It was Stefan who first suggested Jake should become a partner in the business, and that was how he became even more involved, although by then his own business interests in London were rapidly expanding.

Jake's father, John Adams, had also re-married, shortly after the divorce. His new wife, Alicia, was the only child of a wealthy shop owner in Marseilles. She'd been a young French student when they'd first met and knew when she'd finished her studies she would have to return to France. As her father was getting old, and she had no brothers or sisters, she would be the one to take over the business. After falling in love with John, she'd persuaded him to go with her to visit her father. Once there, and seeing his daughter looking happy, he asked John to take over the business with Alicia so he could retire. This arrangement suited John. Within a short time, he was married and had fathered

Daniel and was at last living in France, in the manner to which he'd always aspired.

Jake loved his new stepmother equally as much as he loved his new stepfather, Stefano, and his half-brother Daniel, who was only a few months older than Sara. As his two half siblings grew up it was quite natural for Jake to become the much adored older brother to them both, a role he enjoyed immensely.

But all this meant very little to Jake at that moment, because by the end of the evening he'd begun to feel apprehensive about his life in general, fearing it was going off in a direction he wasn't happy with. His big problem was he didn't know Jane had seen him with Sara, or that she'd already added up the numbers, sure to have given her the wrong answer. Jake unfortunately, was quite right to be afraid.

Meanwhile, the lady in question was in New York, using her natural talent for teaching, doing what she did best, training colleagues. This particular training session was one of many her sick colleague had been running for several weeks, with more weeks at different locations throughout the states still to go, when she'd been rushed to hospital and Jane had been co-opted to take over.

Jane had no option but to manage the best she could. After the first day she knew she would enjoy the courses. They'd been so well researched and programmed it was easy to take over; Jane's only problem was knowing Jake had another woman in his life and, being so far away, she couldn't do anything about it until she returned home. She had to be pragmatic and soldier on, regardless and deal with his infidelity at a later date. In the meantime, he would have to take care of himself, as he obviously didn't need her, or her love!

Jane did manage to leave a message for her father who, to her surprise was not available for a few days, or so his secretary told her. As for Jessie, the office receptionist told her she too was on a couple of days leave, which seemed strange, as she'd made no mention of taking a holiday before Jane had left! Even Jake was still missing, gone abroad on business, so his secretary told her, she too unable to say exactly where. To Jane's over active mind all she could think was Jake was no doubt tucked up in bed somewhere with his new ladylove.

With the pressure of her own job to think about, she knew her personal life would have to take second place until she arrived home, hoping there wouldn't be too many broken pieces from her marriage for her to pick up and salvage.

Having been coerced into an arranged marriage with someone she didn't really know hadn't been her ideal way of choosing a husband but, until the other day, she thought she might have struck lucky in having Jake as her husband. Unfortunately, it now it looked as though her marriage might be over!

There was no doubt she missed him. He was constantly on her mind, even though she knew she must forget him for a while as work came first at the moment. Even then, as she tried to fall asleep in the enormous hotel bed, she longed to be in his arms and for them to be making love.

No matter that she'd seen him with another woman, her traitorous body still yearned for him, wanting desperately for him to make love to her in his own inimitable way, even if he didn't love her?

Chapter Eleven

Oblivious to the problems Jake and Jane were having, Jessie was eagerly impatient as she waited for Andrew to arrive. Within seconds of him entering her flat she was in his arms, kissing him soundly, with Andrew debating whether, instead of taking her out for a meal, he should be taking her to bed! Curbing his lust for later, they went out to eat where, once they'd eaten their first course, Andrew took a ring box out of his pocket. He might have proposed to her a few days earlier, but having an engagement ring had never occurred to Jessie, until now. He opened the box, removed the ring and, with his voice full of emotion held it out to her. 'Darling Jessie' he said, 'I love you so much. Will you marry me?'

Jessie was genuinely surprised and, for a moment or two, she was speechless, words refusing to come out of her mouth. Nodding her head in reply and with her eyes shining with her love and unshed tears of happiness, Andrew took her hand and placed the ring on her finger.

'If you don't like it, we can always change it for one you do!' He said, near to tears himself.

Jessie was stunned, looking at the gold band with its solitaire diamond gleaming at her. 'I'll never change it. It's so beautiful. I'll wear it and treasure it, always.' Her tears threatening to fall as Andrew leant across the table and kissed her, as overcome with his emotions, as was Jessie, both suddenly aware of the applause from the waiters and the other diners in the small restaurant, who'd witnessed the romantic scene.

Later, and slightly tipsy from the champagne the owner had presented them with, they'd walked unsteadily back to Jessie's flat; holding onto Andrew's arm in a way that proclaimed to all and sundry he was her man, a feeling she'd never experienced before. As for Andrew, he felt as though he would burst with pride as he looked at her in the soft glow of the streetlights and, for the first time in many months, he felt content and happy, their engagement sealed later with a bout of lovemaking that gave them both a great deal of satisfaction.

Jake, in the meantime, couldn't believe it was nearly a week since Jane had gone away and he still hadn't heard from her. He appreciated she had her own career and that it involved travelling. He knew from his own experience of working abroad how, at the end of a working day, you just wanted to relax. Then, of course, there were the time differences she would have to cope with. At least it should be easier for her to work in America, partly because at least there, they spoke English, unlike working in Europe where there were many different languages and cultures to be observed. He desperately wanted to speak to her and tell her he loved her. He'd even planned on flying out and joining her, hoping they could talk and perhaps make it a holiday? But seeing Jake was not on Jane's agenda, she was far too busy, and neither was he on her mind, except at the end of the day, when she still hadn't heard from him! She was getting angrier and angrier! First of all, at what she perceived to be his infidelity, and then, even more perverse, that he hadn't been in touch with her! She'd left numerous messages for him to call her, all of which he'd ignored! Was his affair so important he couldn't be bothered to speak to her?

Unfortunately, our star-crossed lovers were being beset with difficulties, caused mostly by other people not passing on messages, like Jake's assistant, who was jealous of his marriage to Jane and quite keen to see them part. Had Jake known of the woman's infatuation, he would have fired her, but of course, this was something he was unaware of at that time!

As for Jane, she thought her sick colleague had booked too many seminars, in too many different places, as she seemed to be spending far too much time travelling between cities, rushing from venue to venue. By the time she got back to whichever hotel she was booked into each evening she felt physically exhausted and her day still wasn't over as she had to prepare for the next day's work, leaving her with no time at all for any relaxation.

After eating a light supper, she would collapse into bed and there she would eventually fall into a sleep that failed to refresh her. With no dreams of Jake, dressed as a pirate, or as a knight in shining armour, or the lovemaking that usually followed, to keep her love for him alive she barely existed.

As an experienced career woman, she was more than capable of working long hours at a time, but for some reason this trip was different; she constantly felt tired and jaded, more than she'd ever felt before, it was as if, somewhere along the way, she'd lost her motivation and her natural ability to inspire others. She put this down to jet lag at first; to her body not yet being adjusted to the time differences as she travelled from state to state, coupled with a feeling of homesickness that in itself was something she'd never experienced before, and then there was her lack of contact with Jake, and her father. She was on a rollercoaster ride of too much work, too little sleep, and no love making with Jake to look forward to.

Several days later, she woke feeling nauseous. After a light breakfast in the hotel's cafeteria she felt a little better, but as she left the hotel she wondered if it was the air-conditioning to blame, or whether the pressures of her work affecting her. It seemed rather odd though if it was the latter, knowing she normally thrived on pressure, but this feeling she had was somehow quite different.

Back in London, Andrew and Jessie, like all new lovers, were totally wrapped up in each other; spending long periods of time in Jessie's king-sized bed, in each other's arms after making love. It was the physical side of being married to a woman he loved that was just one of the many things Andrew missed when Isabel had died. Being an astute and caring person, Jessie knew it was up to her to make Andrew feel happy at being with her and, once he'd overcome his initial feelings of guilt, it would appear in that respect she'd been successful! They spent hours discussing, amongst other things, their future life together. Deciding where they would like to live proved to be the easy part, as Jessie had already made it quite clear she had no desire, or longing, to live in the country. It didn't appeal to her at all. Andrew had thought of selling his half of the house to Jake, but, before that, he had to tell him and Jane he was going to marry Jessie and, like Jessie, he wanted to do that face to face with them both.

Jake, meanwhile was thoroughly miserable without Jane, quietly fuming with anger that he was being thwarted in his efforts to contact her, leaving him to wonder why she hadn't contacted him! And, did she miss him as much as he was missing her? Had Jake known she believed him to be an adulterer he would have laughed? She was his wife and he wanted no other woman, why would he when he knew he loved her. Jane was everything he'd ever wanted in a woman, and the desire to make love with another woman never entered his head, no matter how glamorous the other woman might be. Poor Jake, he'd gone from being the happiest man alive to the unhappiest and, so far, he didn't know how he could change it?

As for Jane, she couldn't understand what was the matter with her. Each morning she woke feeling nauseous, thinking she might have picked up an infection. By the time she'd showered and had managed to eat something, she usually felt better, but as the days passed, instead of feeling better she began to feel worse! Feeling physically sick was awful; her sickness coupled with her homesickness was affecting her mentally far more than she knew. She'd taken to leaving curt messages on the office answer phone for Jessie: as for getting in touch with Jake, she didn't make any attempt there at all, already convinced he'd probably moved back into his own flat, where she assumed he would have installed his new ladylove. Finally, she made up her mind, it was impossible to do anything about her relationship with her erstwhile husband while she was so far away from home: worrying about her marriage would have to wait until she flew back home, but that was not going to happen for at least another month!

By the end of that week, Jane was feeling pretty grim, her nausea each morning was getting worse, making her rush into the bathroom as soon as she woke, where she had to stay for some time, until it passed, leaving her shaky and feeling off colour for most of the morning. How she was managing to get through her days she hardly knew. By the time she arrived back at the hotel, on one particular day, she decided to visit the hotel doctor and get his opinion as to what could be wrong, just hoping it wasn't anything more sinister than stomach flu!

Sometime later, and in a complete daze, she returned to her room and lay down on the bed. Her head was spinning as she replayed in her mind the conversation she'd just had with the doctor, a middle-aged man with kindly blue eyes and a concerned manner. As she'd sat down, he'd noted her pale face and the dark rings under her eyes; signs of her lack of sleep. He'd asked her the usual questions, such as 'did she think she'd eaten something likely to have upset her? And were other people she was working with also showing similar signs of being ill?' All questions she had to answer in the negative.

The doctor, seeing her wedding ring, presumed she was married and asked if she had any children? Jane assured him she hadn't, as she'd only recently married. It had been his next question that started alarm bells ringing in her head. She told the doctor she wasn't sleeping with her husband at the moment as he was in London; it was at this point the doctor had rubbed his chin in a thoughtful manner, before suggesting she consult her diary for the dates of her menstrual cycle! Jane looked shocked at his suggestion, but did no more than bend down and produce her small personal diary from her handbag and there, sure enough, written in black ink was the answer; she'd had no periods since she'd married Jake.

As she looked at the evidence, her face went even paler, if that was at all possible, leaving the doctor puzzled that a newly married woman should be so surprised, or unhappy, knowing she might be pregnant. Believing she might well faint at any moment, he'd given her a glass of water that she'd sipped slowly, until her colour returned as she waited for his diagnosis to be confirmed.

Jane returned to her room and lay on her bed in total denial. She couldn't possibly be pregnant, the doctor must be wrong, there had to be another reason, but in her heart she knew he was right. Her only problem was how was she going to tell Jake he was going to be a father, especially when he'd obviously decided he wanted to be with another woman?

There were still a further three weeks to go before the training sessions were finished and she could return home and, as she'd sat and thought about her life and the new life she was carrying, she finally made up her mind not to say anything to anyone about her pregnancy until she'd had contact with Jake and told him! Except she had no intention of telling him he was going to be a father, having made up her mind she would start divorce proceedings as soon as she got home, convinced he wouldn't want the encumbrance of a baby if he had a new woman in his life.

Early the next morning, after her usual rush into the bathroom, Jane began to feel a little better. By lunchtime, she was more or less fully recovered from the morning sickness the hotel doctor had told her she might have to suffer for at least the first three or four months of her pregnancy.

To the astonishment of her trainees, Jane ate her way through more food than they thought possible for such a slim young woman.

By the time she was due to fly home, three weeks later, she was already having problems fastening zips and buttons on her skirts and trousers!

Jane arrived back at Heathrow in a quandary, having decided on the flight home not to go back to her flat but, as she collected her luggage she changed her mind again, quite sure Jake wouldn't be there to meet her, even though Jessie knew her arrival date and time, and would probably have informed him. It was obvious he would want to be with his young mistress at his own flat in Chelsea. Her first call, after she'd landed had been to Jessie, who told her Jake had gone abroad on urgent business and would contact her as soon as he could. Jane felt relieved, at least he wouldn't be in London and she could start to make her plans for divorcing him but, at the same time, she was angry at not hearing from him. Ah, such are the vagaries of a pregnant woman's mind!

It was obvious, as soon as she entered her flat Jake hadn't spent much time there as it was exactly as she'd left it. As she started to unpack she began to make plans as to what she had to do next, she had her future, and that of her baby to think of now. A future that didn't include her two timing husband, even though she knew it was definitely Jake's baby she was carrying. Jane didn't intend letting him to know he was going to be a father, at least not until after they were divorced. She was determined he wasn't going to have any claim on her child. All she had to do was to tell her father she wanted a divorce, then get herself the best lawyer in town to help her to disentangle her life from that of Jake Adams.

It's now time for the fates to intervene and play games with Jane and Jake. Unfortunately, these games will have no winners, only losers!

Chapter Twelve

And so began an anxious time for Jane, already in a highly emotional state as her hormones raced through her thickening body. Then there were her irrational thoughts. Utterly convinced by now Jake was an adulterer and she had to divorce him; it was, of course, her hormones fuelling her mind, overriding her normal common sense. Without waiting for Jake's explanation, Jane had already found him guilty.

Her "normal thinking" agenda was completely out of kilter, and had been, ever since she'd fallen pregnant. She was either in a state of abject misery, not wanting to be pregnant or, in high with elation at the prospect of becoming a mother. Another one of her irrational thoughts was her unfounded belief if Jake knew he was going to be a father, he might want her to abort the foetus and this was something she would never do.

Apart from not telling her father, or Jake, of her pregnancy, and her decision to leave him, Jane hadn't even confided in Jessie. She knew she had to tell them soon, or they would be able to see the evidence for themselves with their own eyes, from the way her body was ballooning. She decided to tell them about the baby first, and then, after she'd done that, she would then tell them of her decision to divorce Jake and the reason why!

Life was still difficult, what with the occasional morning sickness and stomach cramps that had started to plague her; also, she cried easily these days, especially when she thought of Jake, and how she'd enjoyed being with him, and the joy making love had given her. In her present state of mind, she was unsure now what to believe. As far as she was concerned there was only one way to conduct a marriage and that was with trust and honesty. To her mind, Jake had done neither! Her own lack of both these qualities never entered her head. It was these double standards of her own that were about to bring her more problems than even she could ever have imagined!

It was depressing thinking about divorcing Jake, but she was determined to go through with it and, once she'd told her father her intention to file for a divorce, she would hold him to his promise to help her, even though she suspected he would now be biased in Jake's favour, especially since Jake had saved his business!

As for Jessie, Jane knew she had to talk to her, even though she appeared to be pre-occupied with her own thoughts these days, maybe she wasn't the one to ask for advice, especially if it was her past relationship playing on her mind, and her distress at knowing the man she'd loved for years was now married to someone else. Of course, nothing could have been further from Jessie's thoughts. She was so engrossed in her love for Andrew she thought of little else, least of all her friend's marriage. Her thoughts were more along the lines of how was she going to tell Jane she'd fallen in love, and with whom?

Jane spent most of the day getting up to speed with Jessie, who was in a real hurry to leave work early that afternoon, as Andrew was due at her flat that evening. Not that she told Jane this. Once she'd left, Jane sat in the office on her own, thinking. By this time everyone else had also left for the day and, with nothing else to do, she made up her mind she would go to Jake's apartment and confront him, face to face, with his other woman.

Later, feeling very apprehensive, she stood outside Jake's front door and waited for an answer to her tentative knock. Her heart raced as she waited: taking deep breaths, she wondered what he would say when he saw her standing outside and, in a perverse kind of way it was a relief when the door remained firmly closed and it became obvious no one was at home. Neither were there any signs of life from the neighbouring apartments. Despondent, Jane returned home, even more determined than ever to return the following morning and confront Jake with his mistress, once and for all! After another restless night, Jane was up early the next morning, intending to arrive at his apartment before he would have to leave for his office. Just as she reached his door, and before she could even knock, the door opened, startling her. To her amazement, instead of seeing Jake, or the gorgeous blonde, a middle-aged woman stood in the doorway. Jane was just about to ask after Jake, and his whereabouts, when the woman volunteered the information that Mr Adams wasn't at home; when questioned further, neither did she know where he'd gone or for how long, just that he'd had to go away on business and wasn't expected back for some time. She was there merely to clean the apartment and, as far as she knew, Mr Adams had never had a young lady staying there! It was obvious the woman was fond of Jake and, after her conversation with her; Jane began to wonder just where it was Jake had gone? He seemed to have completely vanished, leaving her to wonder if he'd taken his ladylove with him.

To her dismay, she spent another evening on her own, mulling over her thoughts, wishing she had someone to talk to. Again she'd been unable to get hold of her father for he too seemed to have gone to ground; as for Jessie, Jane began to suspect she might have found herself a new man and, if so, that was probably the reason why she'd been so distracted of late, no doubt engrossed with him!

The next day at the office seemed to drag by. Jessie was as efficient as ever, even though she was a little distant in her manner; pre-occupied with her own thoughts. Try as she might, Jane had no success in finding out what it was on her friend's mind either!

Jessie put a phone call through to Jane that afternoon from Andrew. He wanted to know if she was all right, apologising for his absence but giving her no explanation as to where he'd been. At least his call gave her the opportunity to find out if he knew where Jake might be, without telling him what her problems were. His answers were just as evasive as Jessie's had been, telling her he only knew Jake had gone to Italy on urgent business and quite possibly wouldn't be back home for some time. He also told her Jake had phoned nearly every day and, from how her father spoke, he knew she was at home. It was apparent her father didn't know Jake had another woman with him, or that their marriage was in trouble. As for Andrew, he'd listened to Jane, knowing from Jessie how moody and distracted she'd become since returning from America; Jessie even speculated it might be the extra weight her friend appeared to have gained whilst being away playing on her mind.

It was then Jessie suddenly had a flash of womanly intuition that she immediately dismissed, saying nothing to Andrew of her suspicions that perhaps there was something else causing her friend's moodiness?

After Andrew had finished his call, Jessie knew it was about time she told Jane she'd fallen in love with him, but the office wasn't the place for heart to heart talks, instead, she invited her to join her for a meal that evening. Her biggest worry was how Jane would feel when she realised her best friend was about to become her stepmother! Would she feel she was usurping the memory of her real mother? It was going to be an evening Jessie could honestly say she was not looking forward to and, from how Andrew had spoken, neither was he!

Pregnancy suited Jane, even considering the occasional sickness and cramps. She stood in front of her full-length mirror and viewed her body from all angles. She could definitely see she'd put on weight, but she wasn't too unhappy with that. She thought she looked more attractive and womanly, especially with the added fullness of her breasts and the roundness on her hips. Her breasts looked luscious, and she could imagine Jake holding them. Her nipples suddenly hardened at the thought and, not to her surprise, she suddenly felt sexy, wanting nothing more than to be making love with him. Even though her body wanted him, she still felt angry at his desertion, and then she remembered his touch on her body: lying on the bed she touched herself, imagining it was Jake and, with her eyes closed, she caressed herself, convinced in her mind, just for a few minutes, that it was Jake's fingers and lips touching her, until she reached an orgasm that left her shuddering and in tears, such was the intensity of her longing for the man she'd married and fallen in love with.

She wiped her eyes and continued dressing, knowing if Jake had walked into her flat at that moment, she would have leapt into his arms and begged him to give up his new ladylove. Was her yearning for his body to be her punishment for loving him as she did?

Jane knew it would be good to go to Jessie's for a meal. She'd always enjoyed her friend's company and, during her lunch break, she'd bought herself a new outfit, one that didn't cut her in half as well as a bottle of champagne for them to open when she told her friend the news of her expected baby.

Meanwhile, Andrew had been warned not to arrive until later, as Jessie wanted to get the meal ready. She even removed her new engagement ring and placed it back into its box, deciding not to wear it until after they'd received Jane's blessing. Being a perceptive man, Andrew understood how Jessie felt, not that it mattered to him whether Jane approved or not. As far as he was concerned, he intended marrying Jessie regardless of whether his daughter approved or not!

Preparations for the meal were well under way by the time Jane arrived. A lasagne was already bubbling away in the oven, with a dish of salad waiting on the side. The table was laid for three, the one detail Jane failed to notice.

She used the bathroom to freshen up and by the time she returned to the lounge Jessie had opened the wine and was just about to pour two glasses when Jane stopped her and asked for water instead. Jessie raised her eyes but made no comment as she went into her kitchenette to finish off the meal. It was unlike Jane to not want a drink of red wine and then the cogs in Jessie's brain suddenly started to churn away, as Jane sat relaxing and sipping at her glass, her mind drifting back and forth from her errant husband to her expected baby, her reverie suddenly broken by the sound of a key being turned in the front door, and then the door opening and her father walking in, putting the key he'd used back into his pocket!

Jessie heard the door and came rushing through, her face flushed; at the same time, Jane's astonishment continued, as she witnessed the manner in which her father and Jessie greeted each other leaving her in no doubt as to their relationship!

Her father had taken Jessie into his arms, in such a manner Jane realised it was far more than a friendly embrace between two friends as he kissed her soundly, before walking across to where she was sitting. Jane stood up and Andrew took her in his arms and kissed her and then, holding her at arm's length, he appraised her, mentally agreeing with Jessie his daughter did look different but in a way he couldn't quite fathom.

'You look as lovely as ever.' He said, smiling at her.

Jane smiled in return, noticing properly his youthful glow. He seemed to be a different person from the one she'd last seen at the railway station only a few months ago. It was obvious her marriage to Jake had released him from the strain of seeing his business disintegrating before his eyes. He was fully rejuvenated, no longer the haggard and worn down man she remembered. At least, she thought, somewhat cynically, one good thing, if nothing else, had come about from her arranged marriage to Jake!

'You look remarkably good yourself,' she said, taking in his new and trendy haircut and the modern casual clothes, and then the penny finally dropped. Andrew and Jessie definitely were an item!

Jane's thoughts were compounded by the look that passed between them, even more so when he'd pulled Jessie into the crook of his arm.

'It must be love!' He said, looking down at Jessie and winking shyly at her, before looking across at Jane and blurting out, 'Jessie and I are going to be married!'

At this point Jane's face was a picture of emotions. Amazement at her father's announcement and stunned that she hadn't guessed.

'You're what?' Was all she managed to stammer?

'We're going to be married.'

'I'm shocked,' she said, but Jane could tell from how they were looking into each other's eyes they didn't care whether she was shocked or not. Jane stood in silence for a moment or two, letting her father's words sink in.

'Are you serious?'

'Of course I'm serious.' Her father said. 'Jessie and I are in love and we're going to get married and we want you to be happy for us and wish us well.'

'Of course I'm happy for you, why wouldn't I be? It's a surprise that's all! I had no idea you were even seeing each other.'

Jane held her arms out to them and held them both, laughing and crying at the same time. 'I couldn't be happier if I'd arranged it myself. How long has this been going on? I must have been asleep not to have noticed.'

'You weren't asleep, darling, you were merely in love yourself.'

At this, Jane said nothing, except to ask when they'd first started their affair. When she knew it had been at her wedding, she knew Jake Adams had a lot to answer for. He'd not only gained a bride, but a father-in-law and a business, as well as a potential new stepmother-in-law. She only wished he'd been with her to enjoy this moment, but sadly that was not to be and, she'd yet to tell the happy couple her own news.

By the time the lasagne was ready, Jessie had fetched her engagement ring and, with a gallant flourish, Andrew had taken it from its box and placed it on her finger, kissing it in a manner that promised much more later when they were on their own.

Jane duly admired the ring and kissed Jessie; delighted her best friend was soon to be her stepmother, intending to tell them her news later, after they'd eaten.

The talk at the table centred on where and when Jessie and her father would get married and, as she listened to them making their plans, Jane was glad her father had found someone at last to share his life with; she knew her mother would have approved of Jessie as she was a gentle and caring person, exactly the right sort of person she would have chosen herself for Andrew.

Jane was adamant they should live in the house in the country, but this wasn't what Jessie wanted. She'd already made it quite clear to Andrew when they'd discussed their future living arrangements that she preferred the city life, with its bright lights and cosmopolitan lifestyle, to that of a house in the country with its Aga cooker and Hunter wellies! Andrew said they would love to use the house for weekends and sometimes, perhaps when Jane and Jake had children he and Jessie would come and stay with them. It was this comment that caught Jane out. Andrew was seated on the old settee with Jessie next to him, his arm around her shoulder, content with each other. There was a lull in their conversation and it was then Jane told them her news that she was expecting a baby.

They were, of course, delighted, as she thought they would be, until they saw the anguish on her face and, instead of jumping up to hold her and congratulate her they fell silent, waiting for an explanation.

'What does Jake think?' Jessie asked, silently hoping all was well with Jane and Jake's marriage.

Jane looked down, afraid to show her emotions, at the same time Andrew squeezed Jessie's arm, aware for the first time of his daughter's misery.

'How does Jake feel about becoming a father?' He asked her softly. 'Is he pleased?' At the same time, wondering why Jake hadn't mentioned it the last time he'd spoken to him.

'He doesn't feel anything because he doesn't know.' Jane answered.

Andrew looked at her, astounded at her tone of voice. 'What do you mean he doesn't know? Why haven't you told him?' And then suddenly he was angry, on Jake's behalf. Angry Jane wasn't including her husband in what should have been a happy event in their lives.

'Because he has another woman and I don't want him to know.'

She said this in such a manner Andrew looked at her sharply. He could see she was upset from the tears that filled her eyes and the catch in her voice, but even the sight of them failed to make him sympathetic.

'I don't want him to stay married to me just because I'm pregnant. It would be disastrous to have to live with a man who would rather be with another woman.'

Jane wiped her eyes.

'Jake must be told.' Andrew said, looking at her closely. 'He is, of course, the father? There isn't anyone else in your life is there?'

'Of course he's the father.' Jane replied, indignantly.

'Then he should be told, whether he has another woman or not.'

Jane cried some more. She hadn't expected her father to be so adamant; she'd fully expected him to be on her side, instead, he'd sided with Jake and, as she sat wiping her eyes, she sat in silence, her heart breaking with her despair.

It was Jessie who took pity on her, giving Andrew a glare that would have been comical in other circumstances.

She moved from his side and sat on the arm of Jane's chair and gently stroked her friend's hair, her tender touch reaching out to Jane, soothing her. At that moment, Jane knew her father had chosen well, Jessie was going to be the perfect stepmother and, holding her friends hand, she tried hard to compose herself.

'What am I to do, Jessie?' She wailed. 'I'm sorry I've spoilt your news. I only wanted to tell you about the baby.' Gulping back her tears she continued. 'Jake can't possibly love me, or be interested in our baby, or he wouldn't have found someone new so soon after we were married. She was with him the first day I met him, I should have known then he wasn't the one for me. It was the night Dad and I went to the hotel for a meal with Leo.'

Jane looked at her father. 'You were in the cloakroom, getting my wrap when Jake walked in with his other woman. He glared at me, and at Leo. He must have thought Leo and I were an item.'

Andrew looked at Jessie, surprised at the venom in Jane's voice as she described that meeting, shocked at how forthright his daughter could be. He knew her to be feisty, but how she was reacting now was something more than that.

'How do you know it's the same woman?'

'I saw him going into his apartment with her the day before I left for New York. They certainly looked more than just friends to me. He had his arm round her and was kissing her. I'm not blind, and neither am I stupid! I can tell when someone's in love?'

Andrew didn't know what to say that would console her, or give her hope that perhaps she'd got it wrong. Perhaps Jake hadn't been unfaithful at all? But with Jane's own evidence of seeing him with another woman, Andrew could do no other than believe her. But, as far as he was concerned, Jake hadn't given any indication anything was wrong with his and Jane's marriage, on the contrary, Andrew would have said it was proving to be successful. If only he knew where Jake was, he'd go and see him and give him a piece of his mind. One thing for sure, when next he spoke to him he would make it his business to find out exactly what was going on and tell him in no uncertain terms what a louse he was to be treating his wife and the mother of his expected child in such a manner!

Relieved at last her father and her best friend, and soon to be stepmother, knew of her expected baby, as well as the state of her marriage, Jane dried her eyes and looked across at her father. She could see his mind working overtime on her problem. She then told him under no circumstances was he to mention to Jake anything she'd told him. He wasn't to tell Jake about the baby, or that she intended seeking a divorce, and certainly not that she'd seen him with another woman!

Andrew wasn't happy with Jane's demands; as far as he was concerned, Jake had the right to know all the facts, and be given the chance of preventing his marriage from disintegrating even more than it already had. And neither did he want Jane to become yet another statistic: a single woman rearing a child without the father being involved in its day-to-day-care!

By the time Jane left Jessie's flat later that evening, the champagne she'd bought still languished in the fridge, at least, she thought, her father and Jessie would have more to discuss later, other than themselves.

That night, Jane dreamt of Jake, once more in his role of a pirate, but this time he made no attempt to rescue her; as for making love to her, he was always just out of her reach, watching her from inside dark shadows. Even in her sleep she wept, until the image of him faded away and she was left clutching her pillow, wet with her tears. Images from her dream haunted her all the next day, leaving her to wonder if this was the fate she was going to face without Jake, to be alone and lonely! Not a life she'd envisaged when she'd said her vows on their wedding day, a day that now seemed a lifetime away.

Chapter Thirteen

It was Jake's mobile phone that had woken him. His first thought that it might be Jane was soon dashed as he recognised his mother's voice. He sat up and swung his legs over the side of the bed, instinctively knowing there must be a problem for her to be calling him so early in the morning.

'What's the matter?' he asked her gently.

'It's Stefano, he's had an accident. He's in hospital.'

'What sort of accident?' Jake asked, afraid from the urgency in his mother's voice of what he was about to hear.

'He's been in a car accident…'

Jake interrupted her. He could hear the distress in her voice. 'Is he dead?' He asked gently.

'No.'

'So, what's happened? Was he driving that old wreck I've told him hundreds of times to get rid of?'

'No. He was in Juno's car.'

Jake could hear his mother weeping. In between sobs, she told him what had happened.

'They were on their way back from Piretti, you know, the lovely little village you like so much. You must remember it. It's where they have the wine festival each year. Juno was driving, too fast of course; he overshot the bend and went crashing down the hillside into the ravine at the bottom of the valley.'

Jake knew the road well, and how dangerous it was. Even Juno knew how dangerous the road was and should have known better than to drink and drive, but it was too late now to voice recriminations to his mother, he would vent his anger at Juno at a later date. 'How are they both?' Jake wanted to know, realising if his stepfather had been killed his mother would have been even more distraught and unable to speak at all. 'What injuries have they suffered?' He asked her gently, wishing he were with her. His mother was a gentle soul, even though she was a steely businesswoman and able to cope with most problems. Stefano was the love of her life and, without him Jake knew his mother's life would collapse.

'Stefano's under sedation,' she said, 'he's broken his back. Juno's broken an arm and a leg and is badly cut and bruised. Unlike Stefan, he hadn't been wearing a seat belt, because he's too fat to do it up. But his size didn't stop him from going through the windscreen, so you can imagine the state he's in! He's lucky to be alive and very lucky the ground was dry. If the ravine had been in flood at the time they would have drowned before they could be rescued and then, according to the police, because the car finally landed on its roof, the police said they were lucky to get out alive, especially as the fuel didn't ignite and burn them to death.'

Jake heard her draw in her breath, in an effort to stop her sobs. He tried to calm her and console her with platitudes that meant very little to her in the state she was in.

'Oh Jake, what am I to do. I need you here. What would I have done if Stefano had been killed? As it is, he's going to be in hospital for weeks, probably months. How am I going to manage without him?'

Jake tried to soothe his mother's fears. 'You're to go to the hospital and stay with Stefan. Forget about the business. I'll be on the next flight out and be with you as soon as I can.'

After Jake's reassurance he would be with her soon, his mother finished her call, leaving Jake pulled in two ways. He'd financed Andrew's company and set it up so it would run now without any financial problems, so that wasn't going to be a worry and in any case, Andrew was at the factory and doing what he'd always done. Jake knew he was merely the financier and could leave Andrew to run the business. He also knew now was the time when his family had to come first, his mother needed him and, for the time being, Jane, her father, and the business would have to wait.

As soon as the line was clear, Jake phoned Andrew, who unfortunately wasn't available, but Jake wasted no time in hunting him down. He simply left a message telling him he had to go away on urgent business and then, booking himself onto the next flight out to Italy he packed his bags, positive Stefano would survive, knowing him to be a tough and strong Italian, both in body and spirit. With Sara living back at home and helping out in the hotel, Jake knew the family business would also survive. It was his mother he was most concerned about, as without her beloved Stefano, she would be lost.

Jake spent the little time he had left before his flight, tidying the flat, mentally preparing not to see it for some time and wondering when he would next be sleeping with Jane. He wondered if she was lonely without him, as he was, without her. But then, perhaps she had her friend, Leo, to keep her company and, not for the first time, Jake felt pangs of jealousy rip through his heart as his imagination started to work overtime, imagining Jane with this other man and wondering if she was already regretting their marriage, even though he had no reason to believe his thoughts.

Jake had the impression Jane enjoyed their sexual activities to the same extent as he had, but perhaps that was only because she was a good actress!

As he finished packing and closed his bag, Jake recalled their last night together. For a few moments he could imagine her, as she'd lain on the bed where his bag now stood ready and packed. Her hair had been spread out like a shining fan, her lovely face with her mesmerising green eyes had been looking up at him, and then she'd wrapped her arms around him, pulling him close, entwining her legs around him, and how she'd caressed him, stroking his manhood until he thought he would explode with his longing and then how he'd felt when they'd finally made love. He'd wanted to die in her arms as he'd pushed himself into her warm body for his final thrust.

His heart ached as he wished for just one more time to be with her, remembering then other times when they'd made love and the way she would kiss him and arch her back as she moaned softly whenever he caressed her gently in her secret place, his fingers bringing her to a fever pitch of excitement as she reached her orgasm and how, in return, she would hold him in a fierce grip with her thighs, as her body worked with his as he'd climaxed; the very thought of their lovemaking gave him an arousal that took until he boarded his flight to completely subside.

It never occurred to him to leave a simple note, explaining the reason for not being there. Just a simple explanation he'd gone to help his mother would have freaked her out, being unaware he even had a mother, let alone one who was very much alive! But a note nevertheless, to say he loved her and missed her would have gone some way to stave off the troubles already piling up for him, it might even have diffused her thoughts that he'd committed adultery, but Jake didn't understand Jane's mind, or her way of thinking, so by the time he'd reached the hotel where his mother and stepfather lived and worked, he'd mentally shaken off his worries concerning their relationship, which was not good news.

Poor Jake, if only his heart ruled his head!

By the time Jake arrived at the hotel, Stefano had regained consciousness in hospital and been x-rayed. Thankfully, his injuries were not as serious as had been first thought. His back was certainly damaged, but not sufficiently for him to be paralysed. Even so it was bad news. The doctors had already decided when he'd recovered sufficiently from the shock and trauma of the accident, he would be moved to a nearby spinal injury unit for more treatment.

To Jake's relief, his mother decided to stay with a friend who lived near to the hospital, to be on hand should Stefano need her, leaving Jake, Sara, and the staff to run the business. Sara had been put under strict orders to obey Jake, without giving him any aggravation as in the past she'd sometimes been inclined to do, but thankfully, since her rescue in London, Jake had become her hero and, for the first time, he had a glimpse of the woman she was destined to become.

It was going to be a case of everyone pulling their weight, if the hotel and restaurant were to continue functioning to the same high standard as before, but Jake was confident from his past experience of working with his mother and Stefano, that he and the others would cope with the present emergency. He just wished Jane were with him, instinctively knowing she would love the hilltop village, with its fantastic views of the medieval towns and villages built on the slopes of the hills that surrounded

130

the area. Perhaps, when Stefano was recovered and back home, they would come and stay, maybe even buy a property nearby, until then, all he had to do was to help his parents, and then, he could sort out his own problems. How the fates must have been laughing at his naivety!

The next day he managed to speak to Andrew, telling him he'd been called away on urgent business and didn't know when he would be returning, without elaborating on where he was, or why. It was a very business-like call, with no enquiries as to Jane, or her whereabouts and giving Andrew no time to ask questions as Jake disconnected the call leaving Andrew staring at the phone, wondering just what was it his son-in-law was up to? Was Jane right in her suspicions he was having an affair?

By the time Andrew and Jessie learnt of Jane's pregnancy, and they'd announced their engagement, Jake had been in Italy for over a week. Stefano was making good progress and was about to be transferred to the specialist unit many miles away. Laura planned on going to stay in a family run guesthouse to be near him, leaving Jake to run the hotel. They were all optimistic for his recovery, even Stefano, which was a good thing, given the severity of his injury and how he wouldn't be walking for some months to come. At this news from the hospital, Jake had shaken his head, for a few moments troubled he hadn't spoken to Jane, distracted from dialling her number by the appearance of his sister, Sara, wanting his attention.

Even Sara's efforts at the hotel had exceeded Jake's expectations. He could see how much she resembled his mother: along with Stefano's charm he knew she would be a prize catch for some lucky young man in the future. He'd settled into working hard himself. Bookings had increased since his last visit and nearly all the rooms in the hotel, as well as those in the converted outbuildings were fully booked, even the spa centre had increased its bookings. Considering the pitiful state of his inheritance, Stefano had worked marvels. Jake had seen for himself that a huge change had taken place, as his stepfather had altered what had once been a jumble of old and semi-derelict buildings they'd first seen, into what now was a very desirable place to stay and relax as the old house had been completely rebuilt by Stefano and the men of the village. Time and effort had gone into keeping all that was historic and then it had been exquisitely furnished and decorated by Laura. The restaurant, like all the other public rooms in the hotel had fabulous views of the countryside. With his mother's wonderful menus now cooked by a professional chef, along with Stefano's extensive wine list, the whole complex was amongst the most feted and popular in the region. It was Stefano's dream to have his business included in all the holiday brochures and magazines as the best and most exclusive place to stay, knowing he needed to grow the business. At Jake's suggestion, a few months ago, he'd purchased even more old houses in the village, planning on making them into self-catering properties, giving the business the expansion it needed, without spoiling the complex or the village. *Perhaps now*, thought Jake, *as he was staying at the hotel they could continue with the project, using his fortune to complete the transformation.*

Once Stefano had started to make good progress at the hospital, Laura returned to stay with Jake at the hotel, mainly to prepare for Stefano's return. He would need extensive physiotherapy for several weeks, which Jake had already organised by employing a private therapist to be on hand. The sooner Stefano was better, the sooner, Jake reasoned, he could return to his life with Jane. But that was going to be a problem, as he still hadn't contacted her, which again was going to be his downfall. Had his mother known any of this she would have been horrified. Aghast, of course, that Jake had married and had not told them, and then that he'd willingly left his wife ignorant of his family without so much as a 'by your leave'.

As for Jane, she was alone and bewildered, positive by now she'd been deserted, and that her short-lived marriage was at an end; equally convinced her husband was deeply involved in a romantic entanglement with another younger and more attractive woman than herself. To say her confidence had been dented was an understatement: it had been thoroughly blighted, leaving her distraught and heartbroken.

The day finally arrived when Stefano was wheeled back into the hotel, just after Jake had phoned Andrew, where, instead of merely enquiring about the business as he normally did, he'd asked about Jane! It was then, in no uncertain terms Andrew told his son-in-law, point blank, to get back home. He didn't ask why he hadn't contacted Jane, neither did he tell him he had a problem looming in the way of a pending divorce, and he certainly didn't tell him about the expected baby, he just hoped Jake was savvy enough to realise Jane wasn't a woman whose feelings could be trifled with. Jake was puzzled, wondering what sort of problem there could possibly be that Andrew thought he should get back home to sort out? There were no problems as far as he was concerned. Jane had been away on business herself and she knew he had to travel abroad on business sometimes as well. He'd left messages telling her so, but hearing the tension in Andrew's voice as he'd been told he needed to return home, and without a good reason, Jake began to think his father-in-law was interfering in his life and told him Jane would have to understand his business came first! Andrew made no comment, except for a grunt, that would have been sufficient explanation for most other men, but to Jake it made no impact whatsoever. As far as Andrew was concerned, if Jake didn't understand it was important for him to speak to Jane, sooner rather than later, then Jake would have to take the consequences for his actions, and he might well find he had no marriage to return to!

As he put his phone down, Jake made himself a promise; as soon as Stefano was sufficiently recovered to oversee the business, he would go back to London, still not convinced, even then, that there was anything amiss with his marriage and that Jane would be there to welcome him with open arms. Poor deluded Jake!

Later that evening, Andrew told Jessie of his talk with Jake. They'd agreed not to tell him of Jane's plans for divorcing him, or that he was to become a father, believing it was better for the young couple to sort out their own problems but that didn't stop them from talking things over between themselves; trying to find a way of getting them back together, without seeming to be interfering in any way. Jessie's suggestion that Andrew should ask Jake about his supposed lover had been met by Andrew telling her it was none of their business, but at this Jessie disagreed, someone had to break the stalemate of the young couple not talking, which seemed to be at the root of Jane's problem. After several minutes of arguing, Andrew eventually agreed, somewhat reluctantly but still not totally convinced by Jessie's argument, that the next time he spoke to Jake he would ask him outright if there was another woman in his life and, if so, what he intended to do about his marriage?

There was a great stubbornness to Jake's nature that Andrew had never seen before. It was this stubbornness that had given Jake the strength in his younger days to excel in his business life. Unfortunately, it was also his biggest weakness, especially when it came to saving his marriage to Jane, who was equally as stubborn! Something Jake hadn't yet realised! She might have been compliant in agreeing to marry him, but he was about to find out his wife could stand up and fight her corner with as much gusto as any prize fighter, and woe betide any man, including her husband, who had other thoughts. So Jake had better beware!

Chapter Fourteen

Stefano came home to a room designed by Laura purely with his recovery in mind. Jake had even arranged for a physiotherapist to live-in and work with him every day, until he was able to walk again, and so it was that Stefano began a gruelling regime of exercise and rest. Even after just a few days, Jake could see Stefano had made some progress and, once he'd got used to his wife bossing him around, he began to take notice of what was happening with the business. This was of course his best therapy, as he hated to think someone else was in control. Within a couple of weeks, he was using his wheelchair like a veteran.

With his mother and Stefano back home, Jake decided he would take time off and go exploring some of the old villages nearby. He'd had no free time for what seemed like weeks while he'd kept the business running but before he could escape he had some calls to make. The first was to Andrew, for his usual update on how the business was faring. There were no problems Andrew couldn't solve and, after a minute or two of general chit chat, Jake casually asked how Jane was?

With an edge to his voice Jake hadn't heard before, Andrew said 'you need to come home Jake. I know it's difficult for you to leave Italy, especially as you have your lady friend with you?'

'What the devil do you mean?' Jake said, aghast and nearly choking at his father-in-law's words.

'Exactly what I've said! There must be another woman in your life if you're so keen to stay. According to your office there are no business deals going on in Italy at the moment that need your personal attention, so if that's the case, there must be another reason why you haven't come home?'

Barely giving Jake time to digest his words, Andrew continued. 'When are you going to come clean and tell Jane she's been usurped?'

Jake was silent for a few minutes as he recovered from Andrew's onslaught. He wanted to laugh; it seemed too ludicrous for words that Andrew should think he had a new woman in his life. It would have been laughable if it hadn't been so serious. Just why had Andrew come to the conclusion he'd got another woman in tow?

'I don't have any idea what you're talking about.' He said, with just a hint of anger in his voice. 'Why would you think I've got another woman here with me? Perhaps you'd better explain?'

Andrew drew breath. He too was angry. He'd been quietly seething for days; ever since Jane had told him and Jessie she thought Jake was having an affair. But he was a reasonable man, and didn't get upset that easily, also there was the fact he liked Jake but his blatant lies were making him see red.

'Jane saw you going into your flat with a young woman on your arm, the same woman she'd seen you with before, at the hotel!'

Jake interrupted him. 'The young woman she'd seen me with at the hotel?' He laughed, suddenly realising it had been Sara Jane had seen him with. If only he'd gone back to her flat the day he'd rescued Sara, and taken her with him. So this was why Jane was avoiding him was it? She'd convinced herself he was having an affair, a problem all down to his own stupidity.

Jake shook his head, unable to believe his problem was of his own making; his only option now was to come clean and tell Andrew the truth.

It looked as if his trip to see the old villages would have to wait awhile as he sorted out his marriage; unfortunately, it was with the wrong person; he needed to talk to Jane!

Andrew listened carefully as Jake told him the reason why he was in Italy. That he was helping his mother and stepfather! It was the mention of Jake's parents that had caused Andrew to draw in his breath, being ignorant of their existence. As Jake continued, telling his father-in-law about Stefano's accident, without elaborating too much, he then told him about the "other woman" Jane had seen him with, explaining she was his half-sister, who on the day in question he'd just met at the station.

136

This, of course, was only half the truth but, as Jake reasoned with himself, Andrew didn't really need to know any more, other than the barest of details, the rest he could learn another time.

Once Andrew knew Jake had a family, he naturally wanted an explanation as to why Jake hadn't told Jane?

Jake was glad he wasn't standing near to Andrew at that time, as he could hear the scorn in the older man's voice, thankful there was some distance between them, as he told him what he needed to know.

At least Andrew felt a little better, once he'd heard Jake's explanation, even the bit where Jake had said, by way of appeasement, he hadn't told Jane because at the time he didn't know if she loved him; when she was sure, he then planned on them having a blessing in the village church!

By this time, Jake's charm had worked its magic, leaving Andrew thinking his son-in-law was a good man at heart and how he'd misjudged him, and really Jane should have no worries, although he did feel bothered Jake hadn't wanted her to know his family before they married! That was the one part that really concerned him. At that point Jake ended the call, before Andrew could probe even more, telling him he would be home soon, just as soon as his stepfather was able to take control of his affairs again. He finished off by asking Andrew to say nothing of their conversation to Jane, as he wanted to tell her in his own way and in his own time.

This disturbed Andrew, as he understood his daughter only too well: he also knew in her pregnant state she was not the normal compliant and reasonable person she'd previously been. But by then the line had gone dead and Andrew had to accept Jake would do as he wanted, it was only then Andrew realised he still hadn't told his son-in-law of the expected baby!

For a while, Andrew felt torn apart by his deception: it was a burden he didn't want to carry, as for not telling Jane that Jake had parents and siblings, that was going to be difficult, knowing he was no good at keeping secrets. He also knew Jessie would prise it out of him, but that too is another story!

Meanwhile, Jane was busy making plans of her own. She'd already made up her mind she was going to file for a divorce.

Her next step was to make an appointment with a lawyer and then she would inform Jake as far as she was concerned their marriage was over!

As for Jake, he was quite happy, thinking he'd managed to convince Andrew not to tell Jane where he was, what he was doing and why. He knew it all depended on Andrew keeping his promise to say nothing, but he was sure being a man, Andrew would be good at keeping a secret! Unfortunately for Jake he didn't know Jessie and Andrew were engaged or that, within a couple of hours of his return, she would have wheedled all his secrets from Andrew. Once she knew the score, Jessie then placed herself in charge of getting Jane and Jake back together again!

And so it came to pass it was Jessie who came up with an idea the next day that sounded so good to Andrew he decided to talk it over with Jake the next time he phoned.

Jessie's plan: to get Jane out to Italy without her telling her it was to meet Jake.

As Jane's work involved travelling abroad, not only training consultants but also assessing hotels for their inclusion in the company's exclusive holiday brochures. Jessie often went with Jane when an assessment was needed. The next morning, while Jane was out of the office, Jessie made a point of doing some surreptitious checking, making sure there were no other hotels in the area where Andrew had told her Jake was staying.

Thankfully, Jake had told Andrew the name of the hotel and even where it was. And as there were no other hotels in the area the company promoted, it should be easy enough to get Jane out there to inspect and assess it, without her realising it belonged to Jake's family. Her only problem was how to arrange it without Jane realising it was just a ruse to get her to meet Jake?

The next day, when Jake called, Andrew told him of Jessie's plan; to his surprise, Jake thought her idea to be inspired, as he'd been trying for years to get Stefano and his mother to move forward with marketing the hotel and its restaurant and holiday complex.

Jessie's plan, Jake was quite sure, could well be the opportunity they'd been looking for. The business would be featured in a high-class brochure and a top-end travel magazine; hopefully resulting in Jane being back where she belonged, in Jake's arms and his life.

Fortunately for Jake, one of his many business friends just happened to be the chairman of Jane's company. After a long and serious talk with Stefano and quite a few tears from his mother, who'd thoroughly berated him for his stupidity in deceiving not only Jane, but also his family, it took only a couple of phone calls, and a letter from Stefano, for Jessie's plan to be hatched.

Stefano had written the letter on a sheet of velum, embossed with the coat of arms he'd inherited; dictated, of course, by Jake, and then sent pronto to the chairman's office in London with their request.

But Jake still wasn't out of trouble. Laura and Stefano had been furious with him when he'd confessed he'd married Jane by blackmailing her, unable to believe the young man they both adored could have sunk so low as to coerce a young woman into believing she had to marry him, or her father's business would be ruined.

Laura couldn't believe what she'd heard, as for Stefano; he'd sat in his wheelchair just listening, then shaking his head at Jake's audacity, equally as baffled as his wife at Jane's naivety in believing him. Whatever was the matter with them both that they could go through an arranged marriage without knowing each other? Good Lord, Stefano had stated, crossing his chest in supplication at taking the Lord's name in vain, they didn't live in a primitive society where arranged marriages were the norm! They were supposed to be civilised. And neither could Laura believe Jake had need of using blackmail to coerce a young woman into his arms, especially if he had indeed fallen in love with her at first sight, as he'd said!

Laura knew she was biased, but surely, her new daughter-in-law must have fallen in love with Jake too, or she wouldn't have married him, or perhaps she would, if she'd only wanted his money?

Jake may not understand women very well before, but after a long and painful conversation with his mother and Stefano, who had to have his say as well, he was a lot nearer to understanding why Jane wasn't talking to him! His mother had cried, exactly as he'd thought she would, as for Stefano, he'd merely looked at Jake, exasperated, that a grown man of Jake's intelligence could be so stupid when it came to falling in love.

With Stefano's comments ringing in his ears, Jake made his way outside into brilliant sunshine, which only served to highlight his dilemma as to how to get his life back on track again. He could imagine Jane sitting in her office, perhaps thinking of him; telling herself marrying in haste and repenting at leisure might well be an apt quotation, as far as she was concerned!

Chapter Fifteen

Jane read through the mail Jessie had stacked on the desk, making brief notes on those needing a reply, until she came to a letter beautifully scripted in black ink on a sheet of expensive cream vellum. It was the aristocratic coat of arms over the name of the hotel that really caught her attention and the very formal English used by the writer. The letter had been forwarded to her, or so the covering letter from head office informed her, requesting she should visit the hotel and assess it for inclusion in the company's brochures. The accompanying letter, from the chairman of her company, asked that she personally supervise the visit? And, if the hotel and holiday complex were up to the company's stringent standards, and hers, she was given carte blanche to do whatever was necessary while she was there, to facilitate the deal!

Jane was taken aback at first; amazed by the confidence the chairman obviously had in her abilities. She knew she was good at her job, but this was an accolade she hadn't been expecting and, all of a sudden, her miserable mood brightened.

As usual, Jessie had sorted through the mail that morning before Jane arrived, knowing Jake had arranged for the letter to be sent. Placing the letter on top of the pile. While Jane was reading, she made a quick call to Andrew to let him know part one of their plan was about to come to fruition.

It was some time before Jane walked into the outer office where Jessie had her desk. 'Can you be available to come to Italy with me for a few days?' she'd asked nonchalantly.

There was nothing unusual in Jane's request, some assessments on large properties abroad needed two people, as it wasn't just the case of an assessor saying 'very nice, we will include such and such property in our brochure!' It was more complicated than that, and this was one assessment the chairman had asked to be done immediately and under her personal scrutiny. Therefore, Jane knew she needed to be well equipped to do her best and, having Jessie at her side, who at first pretended to hesitate, for a few moments, trying not to give away her delight that so far her plan had been successful, when really she loved travelling with Jane.

Viewing properties anywhere, and this one in particular, where the owner used such flamboyant words and the best vellum no less for his stationery, would no doubt be a joy, except for her next thought, this was not going to be a normal visit.

This was going to be a manufactured trip to get Jane and Jake back together, the assessment of the property being merely incidental!

Jessie looked at Jane, who'd been convinced she wouldn't want to leave Andrew, being as they were so much in love, perhaps this visit, to a part of the world she'd never been to before might not be what she wanted to do at this time. Perhaps she wouldn't relish traipsing around the nearby countryside that was always a part of the assessment for whichever hotel they visited, or even maybe just staying away from home! Perhaps she would rather someone else take her place!

Just as Jane was going to suggest that as being a possibility if Jessie wasn't keen on the idea, so Jessie looked up at her and smiled. 'Of course I'll go with you. It will be an adventure! And we haven't had one of those for quite a while, have we? I'll give Andrew a call and let him know. I'm sure he'll be fine with it.'

Later, when Jane called her father and spoke to him she heard him laughing and groaning in mock despair that he wouldn't be seeing his fiancé for a few days. Andrew, of course knew Jake would be waiting for them when they arrived at the airport and it was this that worried him the most. He just hoped the sight of seeing Jake waiting for her wouldn't be too much of a shock for Jane, as at times, over the past week, she'd looked quite delicate, her pregnancy not as trouble-free as Andrew would have liked for her, and it bothered him somewhat that Jake might also get a shock when he found out he was due to become a father. He'd wanted to tell his son-in-law of the expected baby but hadn't, especially after listening to Jessie who'd persuaded him not to interfere. In any case, Jane would be able to tell her husband herself in a day or so, she'd reasoned and with that, Andrew knew he had to keep his mouth closed and say nothing.

Jake's mother, Laura, was a happy lady! Her beloved son was in Italy with her and she would soon be meeting her new daughter-in-law for the first time. She'd been in a great lather of excitement after Jake had sat her and Stefano down and told them of his marriage, even when his sister had been called in to hear the news she'd hardly been able to keep her happiness from bubbling over. She was at the same time both tearful and angry with her son she'd missed seeing him marrying his ladylove, but at the same time, she was happy he'd at last given up his bachelor existence and married. Jake tried, unsuccessfully, to calm his mother down, in between her railing against him for his thoughtlessness and then her eagerness to know what Jane was like; even his brief description of her, and then his meagre explanation as to his motives and his reasons, did little to soothe her, especially when she'd asked him why he hadn't wanted them to know of his marriage, and he'd told her it was in case it didn't work out? He knew from the tone of his mother's voice, even though she was angry with him, she was at the same time hurt, and that upset him more than anything else.

'It was a quick decision to get married.' He said. 'I didn't want Jane to feel she had to stay with me just because she would be afraid of hurting your feelings, had she known you before!'

'I've never heard anything so ridiculous!' Was his mother's appalled comment. 'Girls don't get married these days without being in love!' Staring at him long and hard she continued. 'They have their own careers and they don't need men to keep them, unlike when I was young.'

Jake knew then, until his mother met Jane, he would have no peace. Thank goodness Stefano had agreed with his plan and, later that morning, standing at his stepfather's elbow, Stefano had duly written the letter Jane had just been reading.

Being just a little over three months pregnant, and still suffering from stomach cramps and morning sickness, it was more than a month since Jane had last seen Jake, or had had any form of contact with him. In her fragile mental state, she was convinced her marriage was over, but each time she thought of the word "divorce" she had to fight back tears, at the same time she knew she had to take the first step towards finalising her marriage. She'd gone as far as contacting a local lawyer, one who specialised in divorce and was to keep her first appointment the day before she was due to fly out to Italy.

That first legal meeting had been traumatic. Her lawyer had wanted to know every last detail of her relationship with Jake and her view on what grounds she believed she had for obtaining a divorce? By the time she left his office, Jane was mentally and physically exhausted. She'd tried to be totally honest with the rather stern figure sitting behind a desk piled high with official looking documents. It was an experience she found to be rather intimidating. When she'd explained her matrimonial union was unconventional, in as much as it was an arranged marriage, one of financial convenience: her lawyer's eyebrows had lifted quizzically and, for some time he'd sat and looked at her, saying nothing, just staring at her, long and hard. Being a professional, he made no direct comment as Jane continued to explain how her father had faced ruin and, on his instigation, she'd married Jake Adams only because he'd promised to help her father financially if she agreed to marry him!

Her lawyer looked at her after he'd written down some comments on the yellow legal pad in front of him, comments she couldn't read from where she was sitting, if she had seen them she would have she seen his scrawl as saying, "married under duress?" Along with other cryptic comments only someone with a legal mind would understand.

Once the details of her sham marriage, such as where and when it had taken place, and who had witnessed it etc., had been written down, the lawyer then asked what else had happened. Had she had a normal sexual relationship with the man she called her husband? Had he forced himself on her? And finally, how long had he been gone from her life and did she know where he was?

Jane duly answered all his questions to the best of her knowledge, highly embarrassed at some of the questions he expected her to answer truthfully, except for knowing where Jake was at the present time, because of that she could give no details.

She saw him write one word on the pad, in large enough letters she could read even though the pad was upside down.

It was when she'd deciphered the word, "DESERTED" she started to cry, her tears falling unheeded and unchecked down her cheeks until, by magic, a cup of tea suddenly appeared at her elbow, along with a box of tissues all brought in by a kindly looking middle-aged woman, who Jane took to be the lawyer's secretary.

There were two omissions in her statement of events, one that she believed her husband to be involved with another woman and, secondly, that she was pregnant with his child!

Jane had already made it perfectly clear she wouldn't be making any claim on her husband's considerable wealth; she wasn't interested in his money, at which her lawyer's eyebrows had shot up nearly to his hairline in his surprise. He was more used to young women making large claims on their husband's finances, demanding he pay over the odds for a marriage that had held no benefits to him at all, except for unlimited sex, but that wasn't what Jane intended. She had her own home, it might not be palatial, but she'd bought it herself and it was her only financial asset. She was also more than prepared to bring up her child on her own, with no contribution from Jake.

If he'd already got himself another woman, as she believed, she was in no doubt financing and bringing up a child from a failed marriage wouldn't be something he would want to undertake. Then, of course, there was the fact he might demand she had an abortion! And that certainly wasn't what she had in mind at all.

It was her responsibility to love and care for her child and to provide for it and, thankfully, she didn't need Jake's money to do that.

It was at this point she broke down and cried some more, much to the consternation of the middle-aged man who sat across the desk from her. His thoughtful expression should have warned Jane that withholding vital pieces of information was not in her best interests, but he could see now was not the time to pry any further into the young woman's marriage details. As far as he could see, his client had obviously gone into the marriage willingly enough. She was twenty-five years of age, not what he would consider to be a very young age, and neither did he believe she'd been an innocent and virginal young woman who'd been taken advantage of. And, not for the first time during his interview, did he wonder how different her husband's account of the marriage might be to hers?

Being an astute lawyer though, he wondered what else it was Jane was not telling him. What he wanted to know was, if there were other people involved in their lives, hers, as well as her husbands?

The next morning, Andrew drove the two girls to the airport and waited until their flight had taken off and they were on their way. He shook his head, wondering how it would all turn out, knowing it was up to Jake now to do his best. As far as he was concerned he could do no more, it was out of his hands and up to the fates as to what happened next.

Jane had clung tightly to her father as she'd kissed him goodbye, as if she was never going to return. She looked even paler and sicklier than the day before, belying the fact most women bloomed in pregnancy. He'd even laughed with Jessie that morning as they'd climaxed with their lovemaking, that he would soon be marrying a grandmother! But Jessie couldn't be happier for her friend, she'd seen how much in love Jane had been with Jake and even he'd had the look of a man who'd found the woman of his dreams. It seemed wrong somehow that something should have happened to spoil their happiness in such a short time. As for herself, she would have liked to have had children, but at thirty-eight and not yet married, she didn't expect to be a mother at all. She'd started to laugh as well, when Andrew jokingly called her 'a soon to be grandmother' even if it was only a step grandmother. 'I never thought I would get married,' she'd said, 'and yet here I am, engaged to you and now I'm going to be catapulted straight into granny hood! Whoever would have thought that?'

Jessie had become broody herself when she'd known Jane was pregnant. She'd begun to watch her friend on a daily basis, for the signs of changes an expectant mother experiences, wondering what it must be like to have a baby growing inside your body. She also wondered what Andrew would say if she told him she would like to have a baby with him? Perhaps he would think he was too old to be a father again? Considering Jane was twenty-five years old! But Andrew had been having the very same thoughts. Except he didn't feel old and falling in love with Jessie had certainly given him a new lease of life. He'd even made up his mind should she ever broach the subject seriously he was more than willing to do the deed! First of all, though, he wanted them to be married, as he didn't believe in children being born out of wedlock, but then he was old fashioned in many ways, unlike today's youngsters, they don't worry about being married before they have children! Neither did he want a "shotgun" wedding! He didn't think Jane or Jessie would approve of that at all!

The flight out to Italy was quite pleasant and by the time they landed Jane had recovered from her morning bout of sickness. To Jessie, her friend looked more like her normal pre-pregnancy self.

They walked straight through customs with no problems, and were soon outside the airport main door where a car was supposed to be waiting for them. Jessie saw it first. A silver coloured Fiat "Ulysse", a people carrier, with the hotel's name "Villa Flateri" stencilled on its side.

Jessie had taken control of the trolley with their luggage, leaving Jane to walk ahead into the sunshine, and had therefore been unable to see the expression on her friend's face as she suddenly recognised the man standing by the vehicle's open doors, obviously waiting for them!

All Jessie heard was Jane's sudden gasp as she saw and recognised Jake. The next moment, as she drew level with her, Jessie saw Jane's already pale features change to a deathly pallor and, for a moment, she thought she would have to let go of the trolley and catch her friend, who she could see was just about to fall to the ground in a dead faint!

Jake's eyes had been riveted on Jane from the minute she'd walked into the sunlight. He'd watched her with such longing. He couldn't get enough of her; from her sexy walk and her glorious auburn hair, in a shorter cut than he remembered and then he noticed how pale and drawn she looked. It was like watching a film in slow motion as Jane's eyes suddenly recognised him. To Jake's horror, her body started to sway. It was at this point his senses went into overdrive and he leapt forward, catching her in his arms just as her legs were about to buckle, only just preventing her from falling into a heap on the searing hot pavement.

Jake said nothing. With his mouth set in a grim tight line, that betrayed his thoughts, he held his wife, looking down at her lightweight body lying prone in his arms, wondering what was the matter, surely it couldn't have been her first sight of him, or could it?

Jessie looked across at them. She was in shock herself as she stood next to the luggage trolley, at a loss to know what to do next, since Jane had fainted.

Jake, being Jake, took command of the situation, in his normal decisive manner and, before Jessie knew what was happening, he'd lifted Jane as though she weighed no more than a feather, placing her onto the front seat of the car and fastening her in with the seat belt, all in one smooth movement.

With Jane recovering inside the car, Jake then turned his attention to Jessie who by this time had got herself seated and belted into the back seat. Once the luggage had been stowed, Jake pulled away from the kerb and all without a single word being spoken.

The first thing Jane saw when she came to, was a busy road ahead and then, as she moved her head, she became conscious of being strapped in and could see it was Jake driving the vehicle. What she couldn't understand was why he was driving the vehicle and where was he taking them?

Aware Jane had come round, Jake looked sideways at her, content to leave her to recover, believing the flight, and then the sudden heat as she'd stepped out of the terminal had been responsible for her fainting.

As she slowly recovered, Jane was left wondering what was happening, with only the occasional word passing between Jake and Jessie, as they discussed how long it would be before they arrived at the hotel.

Jane began to take an interest in the passing scenery, surreptitiously giving Jake a sideways glance on one occasion, catching a glimpse of his amber eyes glittering at her, with a look she couldn't understand.

She had a sudden urge for him to stop the car that she might fling herself into his arms and kiss him until they were both breathless. She wanted to explore his finely chiselled features with her fingertips and her lips and then run her fingers through his hair, a shade longer than she remembered, but she couldn't!

Otherwise, he looked exactly the same, except for the tan he'd acquired since being away from her. He was wearing a washed out denim shirt, pale blue in colour and open collared that showed his chest hairs. All Jane wanted was to bury her face into his chest and breathe in his masculinity. The very thought of holding him close made her tremble with desire, as it always had, especially when she caught a waft of his aftershave, its aroma the aphrodisiac she'd missed over the past weeks.

From the colour of his complexion it was obvious he'd been in the sun each day: unlike her skin, its pallor making her look like a porcelain doll.

When Jake had first seen her walking out of the airport, he'd felt exactly as he had the first time he'd seen her walk into her father's office. At that time his heart had suddenly lurched inside his chest cavity and he'd known immediately he was going to marry her: he still felt the same way. He was madly in love with her. He wanted her, but there was something different about her he couldn't quite put his finger on. It wasn't her looks, she was still the same beautiful woman, perhaps it was his imagination playing tricks on him, or maybe he hadn't realised just how much he'd missed her.

As he drove, towards the hotel, aware of her glances, Jake realised just how wrong he'd been, not to tell her he had a family! He vowed, when they were alone he would remedy his omission. He would then explain he had a mother, father, step-mother and step-father and two, half siblings, and then, he would have to confess and explain why he'd not told her of their existence! Afterwards, he would try to make up for his absence in the only way he knew. It might not be easy, but they'd once shared a vigorous and healthy sex life so instinctively he knew that once

Jane was locked in his arms their physical attraction to each other might be all that was needed to make his life right!

As for Jane, by saying she would marry Jake as part of his bargain to help her father, she'd tacitly agreed to have a normal married life with him, one that included a sexual relationship. Giving herself to him had been easy; especially knowing she'd fallen in love with him. She'd even assumed he'd fallen in love with her, from his enjoyment of making love, but she still had the problem of believing he'd fallen in love with another woman and that, as far as she was concerned, was not going to be easy to overcome. Jake had a lot of explaining to do.

Once they were on the open road Jake drove even faster, until they came off the main road and started to climb up the hills, to where the village and hotel were situated.

It was fascinating for Jane, she'd never been to this part of Italy before and to Jake's relief, she immediately fell in love with the area.

Santa Maria, the peaceful Tuscan village soon came into view and, within minutes, Jake was driving up to the main door of the hotel, with Jane wondering what his connection with this place was, and how come he knew she would be arriving that day? It all seemed rather suspicious to her way of thinking. Suddenly she was sure her father had been involved, but why?

As soon as the car stopped and Jake had turned off the ignition, she asked him the whys and wherefores and, after quickly glancing in her direction, he admitted the hotel did indeed belong to his mother and stepfather.

'You have a mother, and a stepfather?' She'd asked, her eyes round with astonishment; her eyebrows rising as her mouth pursed in anticipation of his answer.

'Yes. I have a mother and a stepfather. I also have a father and a stepmother, as well as a half-sister and a half-brother, and lots of assorted aunts, uncles and cousins.'

'And you didn't think to tell me? Do they know about me, or am I a secret as well?'

'Well yes, they do know about you now, but they didn't until a week ago. It isn't what you're thinking.' He started to explain, but Jane was having none of this.

'Is this really how you run your life Jake, by subterfuge and deceit?'

'No Jane, I don't run my life that way, but when certain things happen you have to go with your instinct and mine was to do the most stupid thing ever and not tell you, or them, the truth.'

It took several minutes for him to explain that his stepfather had had a car accident and that he'd had to come out to help his mother run the business that was no longer just a small village restaurant with a small guesthouse but a large and expensive holiday and spa complex.

Sitting beside him, Jane didn't know quite what to believe; but by then it was getting hot in the car and Jake wanted to get them inside the hotel where it was cooler, afraid the heat would upset her again.

Jessie, meanwhile, had been sitting in the back of the car, somewhat intrigued as she'd listened to all Jake had said, wishing at the same time they could have something refreshing to drink and a cooling shower.

The hotel was the most beautiful building, inside and out Jane and Jessie had ever seen and, between them, they'd certainly seen quite a few. The stone used in the renovations matched the original local stone of the village, enhancing the buildings and now, after it had been cleaned, all the stonework gleamed in the sunlight. The main building was an old, yet stylish building, originally the manor house of the village. It blended in with the scenery, as though it had been there forever and even as they walked from where Jake had parked the people carrier, Jane could see the old buildings fitted in perfectly with the original. She couldn't wait to explore the main house and the outbuildings that surrounded it, and then to assess it all, if that was still the reason for her being there.

Jake checked them in at the reception desk and had their bags taken to their rooms, leaving them to rest and enjoy a cooling iced tea on a shaded patio at the back of the building, where the sound of humming insects added to the air of somnolence that surrounded them; without a doubt, they could both have fallen asleep quite easily, it was so calm and serene, a perfect hideaway from the stresses of everyday life. After they'd finished their drinks and Jake had returned, he escorted them to their rooms. Jessie's was the first. Hers was a ground floor room, with an en-suite bathroom and a sitting room that opened out onto a terrace with stunning views of the surrounding countryside, and down to the valley below; its terrace was shaded from the sun by an awning, stretched over a pergola and covered by scented climbing plants. It was idyllic. All Jessie wished for was that Andrew could be with her. Within minutes, she'd undressed and had stretched herself out on the large bed, leaving the patio doors open, allowing a soft breeze to gently waft the curtains. Within minutes of her head resting on the pillows she was sound asleep and dreaming of Andrew.

Jake meanwhile, had opened the door to Jane's room and ushered her in; her cases already set on an ottoman, waiting her attention. He closed the door and, with his eyes never leaving hers, he walked towards her. Her first instinct was to ask him to leave but, before she could say anything, he'd reached out and pulled her into his arms. He said nothing. Placing one hand on her face he turned her towards him and bent to kiss her mouth. Her traitorous body responded and, before she could protest, his lips were on hers: her body pressed into the curve of his arms, her body reacting as it always did whenever he held her. She could feel his arousal against her; at the same time her blood was surging through her as it had always done when confronted by him. Remembering their wedding night, and how it had felt when he'd first claimed her and now, even as she was making plans to divorce him, how she wanted him, not only wanted to be in his arms but to have him inside her; her body clamoured for him. Arching her body into his, she moaned softly, as he caressed her body crying out for him. He removed her top and her bras, releasing her breasts, enlarged by her pregnancy, fondling them, nipping at her nipples, teasing them as they protruded, as though asking for more. He kissed and suckled them as Jane gasped, thinking she would faint with pleasure, sure he would notice the difference, but Jake was too intent on giving pleasure as well as receiving it. Jane stroked his back, urging him to remove his clothes in her wantonness, wanting access to his body, mimicking the way he caressed her. Over and down she went, moving her hands down to his waist and then further down, to his buttocks, loving their firmness until, without hesitating she found his manhood, which, by then, was enlarged and throbbing. Jake removed her hand and lifted her up in his arms before carrying her across the room where he placed her on the bed. Taking his time, he made love to her with rhythmic strokes, bringing her to her climax, before his own.

Jane had moaned, and called out his name, her emotions soaring with the intensity of her orgasm, staggering not only her but also to Jake who, having reached his own climax had wanted to yell and shout out his love for his wife. Unable to believe the depth of his emotions, Jake held her in his arms surreptitiously wiping a tear away from his eyes.

As for Jane, she couldn't believe she'd given in to him so easily. She felt exactly as she had on their wedding night, as though her body had been made just for him, and his for hers!

It was some time later when he made his excuses he would see her later and left her alone, to do as Jessie had done: to stretch out on the king sized bed, leaving the patio doors that went out onto the terrace open, allowing the sheer curtains to flutter and billow in the breeze and for Jane to think of what had just happened, and the reasons why she'd let it happen, especially when she'd decided to divorce him!

Jake had made no enquiries as to why she hadn't been in touch with him; it was as though he lived on another planet, in a place where he could have any woman he wanted without committing himself.

It was some time before Jane woke, this time alone in her room, with the sun already going down. She could hear voices on the terrace as guests enjoyed their pre-dinner drinks. She stretched languorously, sated from her lovemaking with Jake, who'd left her while she slept and gone she knew not where.

Jessie was already waiting in the reception area, talking to Jake when Jane appeared, a transformed woman. She was no longer pale and wan, but appeared vibrant and refreshed, leaving Jessie to wonder if this was perhaps down to Jake, or just an afternoon sleep?

Both women had dressed for the occasion with great care. Jane looking particularly spectacular, wearing an emerald green silk trouser suit, an old favourite, only this evening, the trousers were held together by a large safety pin; thankfully, the matching top covered her thickening waist sufficiently for no one to notice she was pregnant, a fact Jake still didn't know, nor had even guessed.

It was while she'd been dressing Jane realised her call to visit the hotel probably wasn't what it appeared after all. Had Jake masterminded it, if so, why?

Intrigued, she then wondered if his new lady was staying in the hotel as well. Just because they'd made love that afternoon didn't mean he loved her, did it? He'd certainly left her rather speedily she thought, in fact as soon as they'd made love and, from his appearance, she could tell he'd showered! Was that to remove any evidence he'd been with her?

And now she was waiting to be introduced to Jake's mother, her new mother-in-law, how farcical was that?

Chapter Sixteen

Convinced his marriage was back on track, all Jake wanted for his life to be complete, was for Jane to meet his family. After he'd left her room, and before he'd returned to his own in one of the converted barns to get ready for the evening, he'd entered the kitchen and spoken to the chef. The kitchen staff were all busy, preparing the evening's feast, such was the quality of the business.

Jake had already delegated Sara to be in charge of the private dining room and, as he passed the dining room he could see she'd surpassed herself. A large round table had been covered with a white damask cloth with the best silver used for the place settings, along with two small bowls of fresh flowers from the garden, placed in the middle of the table, along with ivory candles just waiting to be lit.

It was going to be a special evening for them all, something Jake suddenly realised he should have organised in the first place, finally understanding he should have had the good sense to introduce Jane to his family first, before rushing her into marriage. Had he done so he wouldn't be facing problems now! But then we are all guilty of hindsight, and Jake was no exception.

With everything nearly ready for the evening's meal, Sara was also looking forward to meeting the woman who'd finally captured her brother's heart. Determined to make a favourable first impression she intended wearing a short linen dress in white. Knowing it would enhance her tan and show off her long, shapely legs. Her dark hair she left free; tumbling over her shoulders, making her look even younger and vibrant, exactly as Jane had first seen her at the restaurant when she'd presumed her to be Jake's lover!

Having made sure everything was as near to perfect as he could make it, Jake waited in the reception lounge for Jane and Jessie to appear.

Jessie was the first, followed a few minutes later by Jane. As she walked into the room, Jake's heart filled with his love for her. She looked so beautiful, stunningly so, yet there was something about her demeanour that was different. He couldn't define what it was, but there was definitely an aura of mystery about her he'd never seen before.

Jane knew she looked good. Once Jake had left her she'd slept for a while, exhausted by their lovemaking, then later, after showering and washing her hair, which now looked like polished mahogany, burnished and gleaming under the soft glow of small lights placed strategically around the room.

She carefully applied her make-up, hoping to hide any vestige of her underlying nervousness. After turning her face into a sensual mask, she donned the emerald green silk trouser suit, a perfect foil for her colouring and, with a final mirror check and trembling slightly, she was ready to face her new family.

Jake walked across the room to meet her, looking straight into her eyes, trying to read what was behind them and failing miserably. He lifted her small and delicate hands to his lips, kissing them lightly aware she wore no rings and wondered why not?

Hand kissing, was a continental gesture Jane thought enchanting, even though it made her want to giggle, but that was no more than a nervous reaction. As for Jake, he looked suave and sophisticated in his formal dinner suit, so different from the man she thought she knew in London.

A few minutes later, a lady entered the room, followed by an aristocratic looking man being pushed in a wheelchair by a male porter. Jane knew immediately the woman, elegantly dressed in a dark blue silk dress and jacket was Jake's mother; he'd inherited not only her good looks, but also her colouring; amber eyes and dark hair, speckled with silver threads. Taking Jane by the hand, he walked her across the room to introduce the two women he loved to each other.

Not until his mother and Stefano had finished welcoming Jane into the family, with much kissing and gesticulating, as only an Italian family can do, did Sara move out of the shadows and step forward.

Jane gasped, immediately recognising the young woman standing in front of her. Her first instinct was to slap the young woman's face, believing her to be her love rival, but at the same time her heart leapt, her stomach recoiling with jealousy, faced as she was with Jake's lover, looking even younger in the flesh than when Jane had first seen her!

For a moment she was dumbstruck, wanting only to ask why she was being introduced to his mistress, but the words never left her mouth. She was vocally paralysed, her indignation and temper rising as colour flamed her throat and cheeks. Just as suddenly, her colour drained away, leaving her pale and drawn. In her confused state Jane was even more shocked when, to her utter surprise, Jake introduced the young woman as his sister!

A mass of emotions flooded over her and, for a few moments she couldn't believe what she was hearing, until at last his words penetrated her fogged brain. Was it true? Did she really hear Jake say the young woman was his sister? She couldn't be sure. The young woman stood in front of her with Jake's arm around her shoulders, both looking anxiously at her.

'This minx has,' said Jake, 'unknowingly been the cause of some grief to both of us.' He looked deeply into Jane's eyes, willing her to understand.

For a moment or two Jane looked away, trying to control her emotions, unsure of herself, at the same time ashamed, as she realised she'd made a big mistake in her misjudgement of her husband!

It was then Jane saw Sara for what she was, a young woman, barely out of her teens and certainly not her husband's mistress! How could she have thought Jake had been unfaithful to her? She'd done him a great injustice and, for the first time, she realised just how foolish she'd been, jumping to conclusions without any evidence, except that of her own vivid imagination.

In a conciliatory gesture Sara didn't quite understand at first, Jane reached out and drew the young woman into her arms, kissing her gently on both cheeks, her gesture speaking volumes, as she told the young woman how happy she was to meet her and, truthfully, how she'd always wanted a sister. It was at that moment their friendship was sealed; from then on, Sara became one of Jane's most fervent admirers and later, her champion.

With the introductions made, Jake's mother led the way into the private dining room, with Stefano following in his wheelchair and with Jake keeping a tight hold on Jane's arm, afraid she would vanish from his sight if he let her go.

The meal that evening was everything Jane expected of a high-class restaurant serving discerning diners. All the courses were divine; with all the specialities of the region cooked and served to perfection and served with Stefano's finest wines. When she commented to Jake on the lavishness of the meal he assured her this was just an everyday meal they served to the cliental, at which Jane raised her eyes and made no comment. This certainly was fine dining at its best and, if this was the normal quality of the food, and the manner in which it was served, then she would have to give the restaurant her highest accolade when it came to assessing it, if that was what she was still expected to do, having seen through the ruse that had brought her and Jessie here.

After they'd eaten and the table had been cleared, Stefano made a speech welcoming Jane and Jessie to his home and to Italy, his words allaying some of Jane's fears as he extolled Jake's virtues, with much laughter from those at the table who knew him well, with a wink in her direction and the comment that a favourable report on the complex would be in her interest as well as his!

Jake had found Jane's hand under the cover of the tablecloth and squeezed it; he didn't care personally whether the report was good or bad, especially as it had merely been a ruse to get her to come out to Italy. As it had had the desired effect, that was all that mattered to him. Now she was with him and it was his intention for her to be back in his arms later, where she belonged and, whatever had happened to cause a rift between them he intended to erase from her mind, in the only way he knew how? He'd made no mention of spending the night with her, but it was obvious from the attention he gave her for the rest of the evening, and how he'd held her arm as he'd escorted her and Jessie to their rooms it was his intention to do just that.

As they entered her room, Jane's body ached with her desire for him. Without any preamble, Jake had taken her into his arms. A *frisson* of excitement rushing through her as he started to kiss her, his devoted attention during the meal and afterwards had fuelled her emotionally, leaving her more than ready to participate in making love. Jake was quite sure his emotions were as high as hers as they lusted after each other's bodies, exactly as it had been on their wedding night, both ready and primed for their familiar coupling. They were sexually compatible, with the instinctive coming together of two animals, desperate only to satisfy their primeval sexual urges, and again with no words of love spoken by Jake.

Jake held her close as he started to kiss her. At the same time, she was discreetly trying to undo the safety pin holding the waistband of her trousers closed. As she released the pin, so her trousers fell down, landing in a silken heap on the floor around her ankles, leaving Jake slightly amazed at the speed of her reaction to him. He didn't question it though, merely helping her to remove the rest of her clothes, along with his own, amazed at his dexterity in undoing hooks and eyes.

Once they were both naked, he lifted her effortlessly onto the bed, where he stared down at her, his eyes hungry for the sight of her, his hands roaming over her lush breasts and her slightly swollen belly, until he reached the reddish mound that lay between her legs. Tenderly he traced his way, caressing her with gentle fingertips, engrossed in her body as she was with his, until, at her insistence, Jake finally entered her, climaxing together, with Jane moaning her satisfaction.

They slept that night in each other's arms and, for the first time in weeks, Jane felt her body relax as she slept soundly, unaware as dawn broke of Jake kissing her gently before leaving the bed, pulling a lightweight cover over her naked body.

He had much to do that morning and, because of this, he didn't witness his wife's early morning sickness. By the time she saw him again, much later in the day, she'd recovered and, once again, Jake was unaware of his impending journey into fatherhood.

Jane and Jessie spent most of the morning viewing the hotel, along with the barns and outbuildings already converted into suites and then, after a light lunch, and a short siesta, they viewed the grounds. From a business point of view, they'd done most of the preliminary work, discussing their findings and agreeing this was a very special place. By then it was time for them to return to their rooms to change and dress for yet another special dinner Jake's mother had organised.

Laura had interrupted them during the afternoon to remind them of the dinner they were having that evening. This was to be a special meal for her and Stefano's friends, as well as their business associates. It was also to celebrate Jane and Jake's marriage. It wasn't going to be too formal an occasion, but dressing up would be expected.

All Jane really wanted was a shower, and to cool down after spending the day in the sun, and then to curl up in bed after a light supper and sleep, but she knew this wasn't going to be an option that evening. She did manage a short rest though before dressing, trying to cover her tiredness with extra make-up but even that didn't completely hide how she was feeling.

Laura commented when she saw them, on how tired the two young women were looking, leaving Jane to answer they were unused to working in such heat, hoping she would understand if they retired to their beds as soon as was decently proper!

There'd been no sign of Jake all day. Apparently he'd been collecting supplies from the nearby villages, or so his mother had told them, assuring Jane he would be back in time for the planned meal, but by the time Laura began to introduce Jane and Jessie to the guests who had already arrived there was still no sign of Jake.

Jane was talking to one of the local dignitaries when suddenly she felt queasy and began to wonder if she should make a hasty exit to the nearest bathroom, but the feeling passed, as suddenly as it started. When next she looked up, Stefano, in his wheelchair, had come into the room with Jake at his side.

The talk in the dining room that evening was animated. Mostly led by Laura who was excited by Jake's marriage to Jane, who she'd taken an instant liking to. She was bobbing from one group of guests to another, talking of Jane, who was, in her opinion, the ideal woman for her beloved son, unable to resist taking the opportunity to say so to those gathered there that evening.

As soon as they'd finished eating, Laura stood up and proposed a toast to the happy couple. After wishing them much happiness, she suddenly stopped, and laughed. Her dream, she told all the startled guests, was for them to have lots of babies. Jane gulped at her words; quickly looking across at Jessie and then at Jake, who had an expression on his face she couldn't fathom. His mother continued talking, blithely unaware of the thunderous expression on her son's face.

'Don't keep me waiting too long for a grandchild!' She babbled, looking directly at Jake. 'I don't want to be too old to have fun with your little ones. I don't want to be the sort of grandmother who can only sit and watch rather than one who can run around and play games with them!'

Jake didn't look at Jane before he rose to speak, had he done so, he might have given his mother a different answer.

'Jane and I don't want any babies at the moment, thank you mother. We're both too involved with our careers to even think about having children!'

Laura laughed, ignoring her son's remark, but Jane couldn't ignore it. Jake had just said he didn't want babies! To her dismay, she felt her bile rise up in her throat and then, just as suddenly, she was gripped by a pain, so intense and savage it brought tears to her eyes as she clutched at her stomach in agony.

Jessie had been intent on watching the faces of the guests and their reaction as Laura had spoken and just happened to glance across at Jane, wanting to see her reaction at her mother-in-law's gaffe. She suddenly saw her friend's face mould into a grimace, as she struggled to cope with the pain racking her body.

Unable to believe her eyes, Jessie watched as Jane struggled to get to her feet, just managing to put down the glass she'd been holding as she pushed her chair away from the table in her effort to stand up.

The next minute, Jessie saw her double up as another excruciating spasm of pain rushed through her; the next minute, before anyone could stop her Jane had fallen in a heap at Jake's feet.

Near panic ensued in the room as those around her gasped, realising what had happened. A hush fell over the room, broken only by Laura shouting for someone to help, and then Jake shouting back he was quite capable of seeing to his wife himself. Jane lay still on the floor, the pain receding just for a moment, before another, and even more intense pain took its place and overtook her senses, obliterating everything else from her mind, even the loud voices of those who had rushed to her side; a pack of over excited Italians wanting to help, but getting in the way. Jake tried to help her to her feet but it was impossible. Instead, he shoved one of his mother's friends out of the way and scooped her up in his arms. Jessie by now was scared and alarmed. For a moment, she thought Jane had died, she looked so pale and, from the look on Jake's face, he thought so too. His eyes were glittering with unshed tears, his emotions and love obvious to everyone in the room as he held Jane close to his chest. Suddenly, Jane opened her eyes and moaned and, to no one in particular, Jake called for someone to call a doctor. All this happened in seconds but at the time seemed like forever to Jessie, who could only stand and watch.

This was the instruction needed to get the family galvanised into action and, within seconds, Laura was on the phone calling the local doctor.

With Jessie following closely behind, Jake carried Jane through into her bedroom where, with Jessie's help, he began undoing her clothes, removing some; even to Jessie's untrained eyes it was obvious Jane was about to lose her baby, and then she had the sudden thought that perhaps Jake didn't know he was an expectant father, especially as only minutes ago he'd told the audience he didn't want children just yet! No man, knowing he was to become a father could possibly have been as stupid as that, or could he? But of course Jake didn't know!

Jane was too engrossed in her own pain to tell Jake what was wrong with her; as for Jessie, she was too cowardly!

By the time the local doctor arrived, Jane had been extreme discomfort for some time. After his initial examination, the doctor spoke to Jake, who'd never left Jane's side. 'Your wife must go to hospital immediately.'

Jake was baffled as to why Jane had to be admitted, unaware she was miscarrying his child.

'Is that really necessary?' He asked. 'Surely you can just give her something to ease the pain?'

'I'm afraid not. Your wife needs an operation. She is, as you know pregnant, but I believe it to be an ectopic one and sadly, she is now in the process of aborting the child. I must get her into hospital as there is nothing more I can do for her here.'

Jake was stunned. Jane was pregnant and he hadn't known. She hadn't thought him worthy enough to tell him he was to be a father! Suddenly he felt as though his heart had been wrenched out of his chest. Why had he been so convinced his marriage to Jane was safe when she obviously didn't want him to be the father of their child? But then perhaps he wasn't the father: maybe it was Leo, her man friend? Taking him by the arm, the doctor said 'I think it would be for the best if you drove your wife to the hospital. I will call and tell them to prepare for an emergency operation and I will follow you in my car.'

Jake nodded his head, an expression on his face like thunder, he asked Jessie to help Jane and, with no further comment, he went to get the hotel's people carrier ready.

With Jessie's help, Jake manoeuvred Jane into the vehicle, where she could lay down with more ease. With Jessie sitting beside her, and holding her head on her lap, smoothing her hair, the small convoy made its way to the hospital where Jane was operated on within the hour.

Jake sat and waited as Jane lost their baby, without her knowing the torment he was in, only returning to the hotel as soon as Jane had recovered from the operation and was sleeping, telling Jessie he would return to collect her and Jane as soon as the doctors would allow her to travel.

In the meantime, he arranged for Jessie to be given a single room next to Jane's, to be on hand should she want anything.

Jane recovered slowly over the next few days. Jake's absence from her bedside only serving to strengthen her opinion his interest in her only lay in her body; convincing herself his thoughts of her were only when he wanted to satisfy his lustful urges!

The doctor told her there should be no problem with her conceiving another baby, once her body had recovered. Having one ectopic pregnancy, where the baby is growing outside the womb, didn't mean all subsequent pregnancies would go the same way. To Jane's chagrin, she was told to go home and, when she'd fully recovered from her operation, to make more babies with her handsome husband!

Jane was completely distraught, not only had she lost her baby, but also the possibility of having more babies with Jake seemed unlikely, as far as she was concerned. It must be a relief she thought, for Jake, not to be saddled with an unwanted child, having told his mother he wasn't ready yet for fatherhood!

Unfortunately for Jane, her hormones were still running riot through her empty body, making her desire for another child an irrational thought. She knew she was being perverse, but maybe it was just nature's way of filling the void in her mind and body left by losing a child. But how was she to fill the void in her heart, knowing Jake didn't want her, or children?

A day or so later, Jane was allowed to go back to the hotel. She was still deathly pale, listless and certain her marriage to Jake was doomed. Had Jake known Jane's grief was a normal reaction for any woman losing a baby, he might well have shown more affection and concern, but Jane's emotions, as we know, are not a high priority for Jake, especially as he was trying to come to terms with his own loss? Not only his loss of Jane, who he was fully convinced was having an affair with Leo, but his loss of a child that just might have been his, for he'd finally found a spark of paternal love. But how could he help Jane with her needs, when he couldn't understand his own?

Jane walked unaided into the hotel, to be met by Laura, holding out her arms to comfort her. To Laura's dismay, Jane felt like a piece of cold marble in her arms as she held her in a close embrace, her own heartbroken for her lovely daughter-in-law, and for her son, as well as her sorrow at how she'd spoken at the dinner.

Jane let Laura fuss over her, knowing her own mother would have done exactly the same but despite Laura's loving concern, Jane knew she had to get away from the complex, but most of all, she wanted to get away from Jake. She had to think, she told herself. She had to make plans for a life without him because, as far as she was concerned, their marriage was over. Jane knew she loved Jake, and that she always would, but she wanted a husband who could say the words she needed to hear, not a man who wanted her just for sex.

Jake too was miserable, and lonely, unable to confide his feelings to anyone, his repressed upbringing mostly responsible for his lack of feelings. He couldn't focus on anything, other than his own desolation and his thoughts that Jane hadn't loved him enough to tell him she was expecting their child. He'd even convinced himself the child hadn't been his, but the result of her having an affair with Leo. Unable to face her with his suspicions the gulf between them widened into a chasm too wide to bridge. It was at that moment Jake knew his and Jane's marriage had finally disintegrated.

Were the fates laughing at that moment at the mischief they'd caused? Or did they have a solution? If so, only they knew the answer, and they weren't telling!

Chapter Seventeen

On the surface Jane appeared to be recovering from her ordeal to everyone, except to Laura, who could see she was severely depressed. She was trying hard to hide her low spirits, but failing miserably. Laura knew from her own experience of childbirth that post-natal depression was not an uncommon event for new mothers, she also knew without medical attention it could take months for Jane to recover. Worried about her new daughter-in-law, Laura took Jake to one side and told him Jane should go back to London as soon as possible, knowing she would recover faster in more familiar surroundings, unaware their marriage was in danger of being over. Laura just wanted her daughter-in-law well enough to become pregnant again, truly believing a new baby would be the cure her daughter-in-law needed! Something at the time that was the farthest thought in Jane's mind.

As for Jake, he too was at a loss to know what to do. On the surface it seemed Jane was recovering, but as she blatantly ignored him, even when he appeared in the dining room, it was difficult for him to understand what he should do or say. Jessie was also at a loss to know what to say to either of them, shrugging her shoulders in despair and hopelessness, whenever Jake looked in her direction.

Jane spent most of their remaining days in her room, or on the terrace, working on her laptop, intending to finish her report as quickly as possible. Within a few days of being back from hospital, she'd completed her report, leaving Jessie to finalise the legal paperwork, knowing once everything was done, apart from Stefano and Laura's signatures finalising the deal, she was ready to return home.

Jessie of course couldn't wait to get back to London. She'd missed Andrew, who she'd kept fully informed of all that had happened; even to the extent of telling him of her fears that thought Jane's marriage was in serious trouble, and how Jane was punishing not only herself, but Jake as well. All this left Andrew wondering what would happen when Jane came home. Would Jake return with her? Or would he decide to stay in Italy? Jessie couldn't give him an answer. All she knew was the sooner they returned to London, the better.

The next morning, before taking the final contracts into Stefano's office to get them signed, satisfied they'd done a good job, Jane asked Jessie to organise their flights. This was always the best part of any visit, knowing the hotel would soon find the recognition it deserved. Her coming to do this assessment in the first place might have been a sham arrangement, but Jane knew the hotel was every bit as worthy as any other she'd ever seen. It had everything discerning holidaymakers would want, from the stunning views, to comfort at every turn. Wonderful food and wine in the restaurants, and a newly finished spa centre that catered for every kind of beauty treatment known. It was a wonderful business, set in fabulous countryside and Jane could think of nowhere else in Italy that would surpass it, but then she was biased, being part of the family that owned it! As far as she was concerned, Laura and Stefano's hotel would be her benchmark when she made other assessment visits. Her only problem, as wonderful as it was, the Villa Flateri couldn't heal or mend her broken heart. Only time could do that.

The first thing Jane promised herself she would do when they arrived home, would be to contact her lawyer and start the proceedings for her divorce from Jake. She couldn't imagine staying married to him, or living with him ever again, especially since she'd lost their baby. If she ever met another man and fell in love, she would make sure he loved her, and wanted children before agreeing to be married, unlike Jake, who'd married her when he obviously didn't love her. He'd lusted after her, for sure, but that was different, just as he wanted her father's business! He'd wanted the sex part of marriage, which Jane could no longer think of as making love, how could she? Since losing their baby she'd realised she'd merely been used, exactly as she'd used him, unable to get enough of his body. Even now the thought of him acted like an aphrodisiac, as did the very thought of them naked and entwined in each other's arms: lusting after each other, like rutting animals, made her want him. But in her heart she knew it wasn't just the sex she wanted; she wanted him; she loved him and, the saddest part of all, knowing she would always love and want him.

When Jake heard from Jessie they would be leaving the next day and would need transport to get to the airport, he'd acted as if he was uninterested in what happened to either of them. He was coldly polite and withdrawn, merely agreeing to arrange for the hotel's people carrier to be available and that was the last Jessie heard from him that day. He'd kept his distance from Jane as well, after she'd repeatedly ignored him, making no attempt to see her. He'd certainly not shared her bed since she'd returned from hospital. Jane had assumed at first he would be sleeping with her, but when he hadn't approached her, she'd decided he no longer wanted her. From then on they spent their nights alone; two people who couldn't bridge the gulf between them, both convinced their life with each other was over. Jake didn't know what to say or how he felt all because of his childhood therefore he lost any chance of being reconciled with the only woman he'd ever truly loved.

That final morning as Jake and Jessie loaded the people carrier, Laura approached Jane and gently held her in her arms, tearfully saying her goodbyes, the words she wanted to say left unsaid. It would be interfering in her son's marriage if she told Jane her thoughts, and she knew Jake well enough to know she couldn't confront him and tell him he was a fool. She would have to wait for him to come to his senses, as for Jane; she had to recover her health. Laura realised the coldness between Jake and Jane was the result of Jane pining for her lost child. Had she known it was Jake's inability to tell Jane how much he loved and wanted her that was at the root of their problem, she would have been horrified. She'd grown to realise over the years being forced to go to a boarding school at such a young age had stunted Jake's emotional growth, making him lock his emotions away.

Unfortunately, Laura didn't hold the key to opening his heart to release them, only Jane could do that. For that to happen Jake had to change and only then would he find the happiness he was looking for and deserved.

As it turned out, Jake did drive them to the airport. He'd sat stony faced behind the wheel and driven in silence, with Jane sitting next to him, looking out of the window for the whole journey. Jessie sat in the back, wishing there was something she could do or say that would make everything right for them both, but what that should be, she didn't know?

Jake had at least promised Jessie, as he loaded their luggage, that he would return to London as soon as Stefano was well enough to take full control of the business again. Jane made no comment as she overheard his words; he might have been on another planet, as far as she was concerned. She certainly made no attempt to return the brief kiss he'd placed on her averted cheek. Jessie though, he kissed with real affection, his look pleading for her to intervene: a look she chose to ignore, knowing it was more than her life was worth to interfere. Also, Jane was made of stern stuff and wouldn't take kindly to being told what she should do, as Jake was to find out.

Jessie knew her friend could be implacable and totally unreasonable at times, to such an extent once she'd put herself on a course of action, absolutely no one would make her change her mind. To Jake and Jessie's astonishment, just as they were about to walk into the entrance that would lead them directly into the airport departure lounge, Jane reached across and put her arms around Jake's shoulders, giving him a quick peck on his cheek, then hugging him and whispering, 'take care of yourself Jake.' But before he could respond, and hold onto her, she'd walked away and, for the time being, out of his life.

Jane returned to work the next day with a renewed vigour and an energy that amazed Jessie. She was fired up, no doubt running on adrenaline, so much so it didn't take long for them to catch up with the backlog of work waiting for them. Jessie could see for herself Jane had lost the lovely bloom she'd had when she first became pregnant, as well as the small amount of excess weight she'd gained and now, she appeared lean, and hungry for something to happen, but what that would be, Jessie wasn't sure.

Andrew had been waiting for them at the airport when they landed, briefed by Jessie the night before as to what he could and couldn't say. He'd wanted to stay with Jane, but she was having none of that. She told him he could do as he always did and stay with Jessie, she'd said this in such a way the three of them were soon laughing and the tension he'd been expecting, was broken.

Jane wanted to be alone, to relish the peacefulness of her flat. With nothing to remind her of Jake in the rooms, she found she could relax quite easily, except when she went to bed and found she couldn't sleep, unable to erase from her memory of how they used to make love, and then afterwards, how they would fall asleep in each other's arms and wake in the morning both wanting more!

Her first call in the morning was to her lawyer, to ask for the divorce papers to be served on Jake at once. He did, of course, without any success, try to reason with her, asking that they should try mediation first, but Jane was adamant, she wanted a divorce and the sooner the better.

Her lawyer asked her again, on what grounds did she want her divorce? Was it still to be adultery?

As Jake had told her the woman she'd thought to be his lover was in fact his young half-sister Jane knew she would have to have another reason and then suddenly she said, 'unreasonable behaviour,' which seemed in her eyes to fit the bill exactly.

A few days later, Jake opened a letter his mother had placed in front of him; his mouth pursed in a grimace as he saw it was a legal document.

Jake read it through. Unreasonable behaviour indeed! So, Jane was making no legal claim on his wealth, and neither did she want any further contact with him, all future contact was to be through their lawyers.

Since Jane had left, Jake's emotions had taken a battering, leaving him feeling rejected and very sorry for himself. He finished reading the document, and in a rare moment of truthfulness, he showed the letter first to his mother and then Stefano. They'd already witnessed Jake's reaction as he'd been reading the document stating quite clearly Jane wanted to end their marriage.

He'd ranted for a while, declaring he would never agree to a divorce. At the same time as his mother was trying to pacify him, telling him it was Jane's grief at losing their baby, which making her unreasonable. She also told him it was a terrible time for many women for it was when they were at their most vulnerable, with their hormones acting in a crazy manner. Given time, Jane would eventually come to her senses, perhaps then she would realise how wrong she was in leaving him.

Laura went on to tell him Jane was probably suffering with postnatal depression and perhaps he should suggest to Jessie her friend got some treatment. Trying to calm him down even more, she told him because Jane's hormones would still be raging she really wasn't responsible for her actions.

Jake wasn't to be comforted, or reasoned with, especially as he'd started to think Jane might have been keeping something else from him. Perhaps she'd been the one who'd strayed? Maybe she'd found someone else? Perhaps while she'd been in America and the baby had been this other man's, and this was the real reason she now wanted a divorce?

Jake suddenly realised he was thinking of Jane in the same way she'd thought of him when she'd seen him and Sara going into his flat in London? He knew he was being just as irrational, but what else could he think?

Suddenly he made up his mind. If Jane wanted a quick divorce she was going to be sadly disappointed. He didn't intend to make it easy for her to go to her new man. She would have to wait. He wasn't going to sign any papers until he was good and ready! Whenever that might be!

Chapter Eighteen

Jane threw herself into work with a vengeance: taking on more teaching sessions than she normally would, including an extra trip to France to do another assessment. As always, Jessie was left to run the office. The amount of work Jane was doing was more than Jessie thought necessary. Like Andrew, Jessie was becoming increasingly concerned for her friend's health as she was beginning to look extremely thin and gaunt. As the weeks passed, Jane gradually began to slow down the gruelling pace she'd set herself and finally her frantic work life eased a little, until at last, she began to return to being her old self again. Outwardly she appeared to have worked her grief out of her system, accepting she would have to bide her time for her marriage to be legally finalised. The one lesson she'd learnt though over the past weeks was that Jake wasn't prepared be bullied into agreeing to a quick divorce, stubbornly intending to wait a while before signing the paperwork, which didn't seem to be anytime soon! But why, was the one question she asked her lawyer every time they spoke on the phone, but even he couldn't give a reply that satisfied her, having made up his mind months ago that if he'd been Jane's husband he wouldn't be in a hurry to sign the papers either!

It was only Jane who couldn't understand Jake's attitude. To her it was obvious he didn't love her: lusted after her maybe at the beginning, but as for love? No! She was sure he didn't know what the word "love" meant!

Her lawyer's advice was for her to have patience. This of course annoyed her, especially knowing patience wasn't her strongest point!

Occasionally, she would go to Jessie's flat for a meal after work, but even these outings were few and far between these days, although Jake was a frequent guest. The needs of the company demanding he kept in touch with Andrew who, unknown to Jane had taken pity on his son-in-law, inviting him to join them whenever he was in London.

Jake always enquired after Jane's health and her social life at these meetings, but Andrew and Jessie could tell him nothing. Jane no longer confided in them as to what she did in her spare time. All Andrew knew, but didn't tell, was the anger she'd voiced when she'd told him the latest batch of divorce papers sent to Jake were returned yet again, unsigned, with the same note attached *'he wasn't ready, as yet, to finalise his marriage'*. Jane, of course, couldn't understand why he refused to sign. Surely, by now, he must want to move on with his life? But to Andrew and Jessie, apparently not!

They said nothing, having agreed not to discuss the rights and wrongs of Jane and Jake's marriage, especially as Jessie worked with Jane and knew where her loyalties lay, just as Andrew worked with Jake and still relied on him for some financial help; not only that, Andrew liked Jake enormously. He'd never had any qualms about arranging for Jane to marry him and, contrary to what Jane believed, he still thought him to be the ideal husband for her.

Andrew did what he had to. The bottom line was he could have walked away from his business and its financial troubles, but that wasn't how he worked, he had to save the company because too many men relied on their workplace for their living and then of course, Andrew had to earn his own living from the business as well, so when Jake proposed he should marry Jane as part of his agreement to save the company he'd agreed. In fact, he hadn't thought twice about it and neither did he think he was doing wrong. Many a parent in the past had engineered a match between their children when it suited them, especially when a business was involved; also, this wasn't really a cold-blooded action, with no thought for Jane's feelings as he'd seen Jake's face when Jane had walked into the office. He knew what love at first sight felt like; he'd experienced it himself when he'd first met Isabel. Nothing would have parted him from her, but now she was no longer alive he'd had a second chance at love and, having Jessie in his life, was now more important to him now than his business. But thinking of his past was not going get Jake and Jane back together again.

Meanwhile, Andrew's plans to marry Jessie had stalled for the time being. They'd talked it over when Jane first said she was going to divorce Jake, deciding to wait until that was over. With Jake declining to sign the papers it looked as if it could go on for months and months, leaving Andrew disinclined to wait any longer, plus, the delay was depressing Jessie.

Later that particular evening, after they'd made love, Andrew told her it was about time they set a date. It shouldn't matter to them what Jane and Jake decided to do, it was their marriage and therefore their problem!

A few days later, Jane spent the evening with them where the conversation, as usual turned to her problems and the anti-marriage stance she'd taken to holding, ever since she'd returned from Italy. Up until that moment, Andrew had been patient with her, listening to her talk about her frustrations, mostly with Jake's refusal to sign the papers, but that evening Andrew totally lost it. He was fed up with always pussy footing around Jane's feelings, until, quite frankly, he'd had enough, and in no uncertain terms he told her, just because she didn't like marriage, he and Jessie did, and they were planning to get married in a couple of months, implying she could like it or not!

Looking at Jessie's anxious face as her father made his rather abrupt statement, and noting the tone of voice he'd used, Jane suddenly realised it was only her selfish and self-centred attitude preventing them from getting married. They'd been supportive of her and since then she'd been taking them for granted; no wonder her father was sounding more than slightly aggrieved with her. It was only when she'd apologised and told them they must get married as soon as possible, that Jessie and her father visibly began to relax.

From then on, it only took Jessie a few days to make the arrangements for her and Andrew to be married. She came from a close-knit family that included an older brother, whom she wanted to give her away; his young daughter she planned on having as her bridesmaid. She wanted Jane as her matron of honour, but Jane shook her head.

'Jessie, I love you very much and I'm flattered you want me next to you as you marry my father, but I have to say no. The reason is there are so few members of my family left I need to be in the church with the old aunts and uncles.

Of course Jessie understood, and so did Andrew, when Jessie told him. He'd asked Jake to be his best man, but he too had declined, saying he would be abroad on business on the date Andrew had given him, which really saved the day, as Andrew wasn't looking forward to telling Jane if he'd accepted.

Jake did send a rather lovely piece of modern art though, as a wedding gift, a sculpture by Lea Becket, an artist he'd heard Jessie raving about and, along with the gift, he'd sent a promise he would visit them as soon as they returned from their honeymoon.

Andrew decided to live in Jessie's city flat for the time being, spending weekends and holidays in the country house, until they'd decided where to live permanently, which to some extent would depend on Jane, as she owned half share in the house and might one day want to take it over herself, especially if and when she married again, but that was for the future. In the meantime, Andrew decided they would get married in the old church in his home village, with a reception held afterwards in a marquee in the large garden of the house.

Although they frequently shared a bed in her flat, so far they'd never shared a bed at Andrew's house; it didn't seem right somehow to Jessie to share what had once been Isabel's bed with him until they were married. Ever mindful of how she felt, Andrew had removed all the furniture and redecorated the room, giving her free reign over how it should be furnished and decorated. So the night before the wedding Jessie stayed in a local hotel with her brother and his family, as for Jane, she slept in her old room, in the antique four-poster that had been hers since she'd been ten years old.

Disturbed by the activity in the garden Jane woke early and, as she looked out of her bedroom window, she could see it was going to be a sunny day now the early morning mist had cleared.

The next minute a van pulled up on the drive and soon there was a bevy of men carrying tables and gilt chairs into the marquee, quickly followed by the local florist, his arms full of boxes of flowers and containers that would soon transform the marquee into a grand salon.

By two o'clock the workmen had left, leaving the marquee ready for the caterers to get the food organised. An hour later, the church was already filled with Andrew and Jessie's families and friends, along with most of the villagers waiting for the wedding to start.

Jane, accompanied by her father and Sir Ernest, was the first to walk through the lych-gate up the path to the church. A minute or so later, Jessie, always punctual, well nearly always, arrived. According to the clock on the bell tower it was exactly three o'clock.

The bride looked radiant, dressed as she was in a traditional cream brocade wedding dress, with its sweetheart neckline, long pointed sleeves with a row of small covered buttons going up the inside of the arm and a train, that fanned out behind her as she walked down the aisle on her brother's arm, to join her groom, who'd been standing in front of the altar patiently waiting.

Andrew looked resplendent in his morning suit, as he waited. Turning to look at Jessie as she neared to where he was standing, his heart nearly bursting with his love for her.

Jessie looked beautiful; her blonde hair had been styled into a chignon, with a pearl studded headdress and a short veil setting it off perfectly. In her arms she carried a small sheaf of white arum lilies, hand-tied with a cream silk ribbon that trailed elegantly down the front of her dress.

Her one small bridesmaid looked charming, dressed in pale lavender tulle. Her headdress, along with the small posy of silk flowers she carried, had been made in varying shades of pale blue and lilac and, as she followed behind Jessie, there wasn't a dry eye in the congregation.

Sir Ernest, Andrew's best man, did his part in the ceremony too, by handing over the matching gold wedding rings to be blessed before they were placed on Jessie and Andrew's fingers and then later, at the reception, in his role as best man he made a speech that had everyone crying with laughter, but best not repeated here.

It was a lovely family wedding that even in her depressed state Jane had enjoyed. It brought back memories of her marriage to Jake, even though that had been a much simpler affair and in a setting totally different from her fathers. She could still remember how she'd felt when Jake had placed her wedding ring on her finger and the way he'd kissed her ring and looked at her. Now she wore no rings at all. They were locked away, never to see the light of day ever again as far as she was concerned.

Andrew had organised all the entertainment for the reception, as well as the evening entertainment. First of all, a string quartet was to play while they were eating. And then, after the wedding cake had been cut and the speeches and toasts had been made, there was to be a break in the proceedings while the tables were moved aside to allow more room for dancing. At this point, the old aunts and uncles went into the house and rested, while Jane and Jessie changed into dresses more suitable for dancing.

Once the marquee had been transformed into a replica nightclub, with a local man acting as DJ, and a small local band had set up their gear, everyone trooped back to enjoy the rest of the evening.

Andrew and Jessie started off the evening's entertainment with a waltz, their first as man and wife and, from then on, the evening went with a swing, especially the disco session for the young ones. And then the band started playing a selection of old and favourite songs. To Jane's surprise, nearly everyone took to the floor and danced until it was time for a late supper.

Just after midnight, Andrew told those that were left, it was time for him and his bride to retire and then, when everyone had gone, except for Jane, they spent their first night in the house in the newly decorated bedroom, heading off early the next day on a honeymoon, that to Jessie was at an unknown destination.

Meanwhile Jake had been working hard back in Italy, trying to forget Jane. So far, he hadn't managed it as she was always on his mind.

He'd gone back thinking working with his hands might help. He'd supervised the decoration of some new studios and apartments he and Stefano had had built in the old village houses.

Stefano was now back at work and mostly recovered, but under strict instructions from Laura to rest each afternoon, which of course he didn't object to obeying, especially if it meant he could spend an hour or more with his wife, who was still his lover.

Jake knew how much his mother hated Jane wanting a divorce. She couldn't understand why, as they'd seemed so suited to each other, even from the little she'd seen of them, but then, perhaps it was just her mother's instinct homing in on their body language, more than what they said?

It had been her idea for Jake to stall signing the documents and not immediately returning them as Jane's lawyer had requested. Her reasoning being, given time, Jane might realise just how much she loved Jake and perhaps then, she might be prepared give their marriage a second chance. After a while, even Laura had to admit it was unlikely Jake would ever see his wife again. But on this count they were both wrong.

Jake, on a fleeting visit, had only been back in London for one day when he just happened to see Jane, arm in arm with the same man he'd seen her with at the airport, crossing Oxford Street. Immediately, his thoughts that she did have another man in tow appeared to be true. He'd stopped and watched as they disappeared into the entrance of a hotel, leaving Jake angry to the point where he wanted to follow them and confront the man in question.

These feelings of anger and jealousy rose up inside Jake to such an extent, he wanted to challenge them to come clean about their relationship; thankfully though, common sense prevailed, leaving him fuming on the opposite side of the street, with Jane ignorant of what he'd thought he'd seen.

The next day he went to see Andrew and, even before he'd asked after Jessie, or the business, he demanded to know whether Jane had a new man in her life, and if so who was he?

Andrew had been taken aback at Jake's anger, shaking his head, as baffled as he looked and wondering why his soon to be ex son-in-law should think as he did. He could see for himself Jake was extremely angry, even when he'd told him he didn't think Jane had time to find another man, as she was too busy with her work.

Andrew could see his words were having little or no effect on Jake's thinking. No matter what he said Jake was still not convinced. His parting words to Andrew were he would continue to refuse to sign the divorce papers, as he was sure Jane had another man in her life and, maybe he should tell his solicitor he wasn't the unreasonable one in the marriage! It was Jane who was an adulteress!

When Andrew repeated Jake's comment to Jane later it had left her fuming. As for Jake, by then, he'd taken himself back to Italy leaving Jane was in no doubt his refusal to sign was just because of some perverse reason she didn't understand. It had nothing to do with his supposed theory she had another man in tow. He just wanted to hold onto her, but why? He obviously didn't love her, or he wouldn't have rejected her in front of his mother, stepfather and the other guests when he'd stated he didn't want children!

It was this single comment Jane had taken as his rejection of her; as for their marriage, from then on it had been doomed.

As for his mother wanting her to have another baby with Jake, as far as Jane was concerned that just wasn't going to happen!

Jane had decided there would be no more babies for her until she found herself a man who really loved her for herself, not for some ill-gotten material gain.

And, never again would she enter into a marriage of convenience!

Chapter Nineteen

Jane's oldest friends, Sylvie and Leo, were due to leave their suburban house in Surrey to live in New York for a couple of years. As Leo was to take up a new position as Deputy Head of Finance for the American arm of the company he'd worked for in London. It was a five-year contract to start with, and a wonderful opportunity for him. It was a promotion he'd dreamt of, but there was a downside. Sylvie wasn't looking forward to leaving her family and friends behind, and especially Jane, who was still not fully recovered from the loss of her baby and the break-up of her marriage. The morning Jake happened to see Jane with Leo had been the last time Sylvie had seen Jane. The three of them had met up for a farewell lunch. As they were all old friends, it was quite natural for Leo to give Jane his arm to hold as they walked along, especially since she'd been so unwell. It was just too bad Jake happened to see Jane laughing up at Leo, as if he'd said something amusing: it was this one action on Leo's part that resulted in Jake being convinced he was rightly justified in not signing the divorce papers. His attitude being, if he couldn't have Jane, then no one else would either! Of course it was natural after this for Jake to cast Leo in the role of the baddie, when in fact he was anything but. To Jane, Leo was the brother she'd never had, as well as being her best friend's husband. Neither was he the type of man she would have ever fallen in love with, but of course Jake didn't know this. All he knew were the agonies he was experiencing. If he'd known Leo was the love of Sylvie's life, things might have been different and, if Leo had been at their wedding and had met Jake, perhaps it would all have worked out differently, but really it certainly seemed as though the fates were looking for any way to inflict more pain on him, determined he should pay dearly for his rejection of Jane.

Jake went to see Andrew and Jessie one evening, his first visit since they'd returned from their honeymoon. To his surprise, there had been no mention of Jane at all during the meal, wondering if all was well with her, he casually asked after her. It was Jessie who answered, after giving a warning glance in Andrew's direction he understood to mean he should keep quiet. Taking her time, and leaning forward, Jessie at first concentrated on pouring more wine into Jake's glass.

While on honeymoon, she and Andrew had come up with a plan to bring the erstwhile lovers together. They'd agreed they were interfering, but had decided they had no other choice. Whatever they did they were on rocky ground, knowing any plan they thought of had only a small chance of being successful; but what they did know was they needed to get them both in the same place at the same time. Then, if they did love each other, there was a good possibility they would fall into each other's arms! This had sounded too good to work when they'd first hatched their plan. Being "loved up" themselves and lying on the golden sand of their honeymoon resort, with the sun beating down on them and after they'd drunk several glasses of sangria. It had seemed like a good idea at the time except for the biggest problem? Putting their thoughts into actions would be the hardest part.

Jessie looked up from pouring the wine. 'Jane's fine. She's in love, you know?'

The look on Andrew's face nearly had her choking on her suppressed laughter.

As for Jake, he said nothing. Jessie had given him the answer he'd been dreading, yet, at the same time the one he'd been expecting, especially after he'd seen Jane with another man.

He felt as though he'd been punched in the stomach, his breath knocked out of him.

Jessie watched Jake's face at it betrayed his emotions, wondering if he would express his curiosity and ask if she knew who it was Jane was in love with. From his bleak expression it was apparent he didn't want to know. He looked too upset, but Jessie wasn't finished, not yet. This was the moment she'd been waiting for.

'Yes, she's in love, but the man she's in love with has a problem.'

At this, Jake jerked his head up and stared at her intently; convinced she was going to name the man he'd seen her with.

'What sort of problem?' He asked, but Jessie remained tantalisingly silent.

She waited for a moment longer and then looked across at Andrew who was sitting hunched in his seat, waiting for Jake to explode with anger.

'The man she's in love with doesn't know how to tell her he loves her!

He finds it hard to say those three little words that mean so much to a woman?'

Jake looked stunned. 'What do you mean? Who is the man Jessie? Tell me!'

'Jake, it's you! You are an idiot! You're the man she loves, but do you love her?'

'Jessie, I not only love her, I adore her.' He snapped back.

'Am I going mad?' He asked Andrew who by now was wondering if Jessie had gone too far!

'I can't answer that!' He said.

Jessie laughed. 'So why didn't you tell her then?'

But Jake couldn't answer. He hung his head in embarrassment as the colour crept up his neck and into his face. After a few moments he looked up, turning from one to the other, his look lingering on Andrew, hoping to see some sign of support from a fellow male, but Andrew gave him no sign at all as to how he could extricate himself from further humiliation at Jessie's hand.

Andrew's refusal to help was apparent, it signalled to Jake this was one project where he was on his own. This was his problem. Andrew could see Jake had kept his emotions locked up inside him for so long that opening up to anyone was going to be difficult. Taking pity on him at last, Andrew smiled, an encouraging smile. It was just a small sign, but it showed male solidarity and, thankfully, it was all Jake needed. Before he knew what was happening he was talking to them both, blurting out his angst.

'I know I'm no good at expressing my feelings. But that doesn't mean I don't have any, because I do.'

Jessie let him talk. Suddenly it was as though the floodgates had opened and at last Jake knew it was what he'd needed to do for years. He had to accept his feelings were as normal and as valid as anyone else's. Saying what was in his heart was important. Before he knew what was happening, Jessie and Andrew knew more about Jake than they'd ever bargained for. It was Jessie's gift of being able to analyse feelings and emotions that was going to help Jake; more than many sessions with a therapist could ever do.

Jessie told him, in no uncertain terms he'd been a fool and for once Jake agreed. He knew he hadn't really taken to heart what Liza and Mark had tried to show him, he'd only listened to what Liza had said about wooing a woman with gifts, material things Jane didn't need or want. He knew that now. Then Jessie asked him how could the simple equation of him being in love with Jane, and her being in love with him, be so difficult for them both to understand, acknowledge and not get right?

Jake shook his head. He didn't know how to answer, and then it came out in a rush, 'it's Jane who wants the divorce. Not me. She's adamant about that. I've even tried not signing or returning the papers but I can't do that for much longer. My lawyer tells me I must sign and let the marriage end, but I don't want to do that. I know once they're signed, that will be it! It will be finished and I will have lost her for ever.'

It was obvious Jake was at last admitting defeat. He'd prevaricated for far too long. As for seeing Jane again, or her ever agreeing to be alone with him, or even getting her to listen to him as he tried to convince her he loved her, wasn't something he could imagine ever happening.

'Well, you've got a new mother-in-law now who's going to help you,' said Jessie, 'so you'd better listen carefully and we'll see if we can't get you both together again?'

Just how she was going to do this Jessie had yet to think. It was going to take something like a minor miracle but, as Jake returned to his flat later he was at least convinced Jessie might well be the only person who could make the miracle happen and, for the first time in months, he felt more optimistic than he'd been in a long while.

It was a day or so later when Jessie managed to speak to Jane. Talking as women do with each other, and in a way men rarely understand.

Jessie's relationship, as her new stepmother gave her an edge on asking personal questions. In fact, Jessie asked Jane outright to explain exactly what had been the cause of her marriage spilt with Jake? She knew it wasn't just the loss of the baby that was bad enough, so there must be something else that had happened before then, something Jane hadn't spoken about, because to Jessie's mind they'd seemed so happy and in love before Jane had gone to America, regardless whether Jake had denied Jane didn't love him!

Jessie knew the marriage had been arranged in the first instance to save Andrew's company from closing. She had already remonstrated with her new husband about his ethics. It was then, to her surprise, Andrew had told her what had happened the day Jane and Jake had first met.

'Jessie, you wouldn't believe how electric the air was when Jane walked into the room. They both took one look at each other and you could hear the electricity between them crackling. It was a magical moment for me as well, even though I was only looking on, so how they must have been feeling I can't imagine. When Jake said later he would help me only if Jane agreed to marry him I thought it would be a good idea. They seemed so suited to each other. She refused, of course, and I can't say I blamed her because Jake hadn't a clue how to woo a woman. I'm just surprised he ever managed to get a woman into bed before he saw Jane, as for romantic talk, well, as far as I can tell, Jake doesn't do romance!'

'But he bought her a beautiful engagement ring and wedding ring, without any help from anyone and I know he bombarded her with flowers and perfume...' said Jessie. Her eyes filling with tears, she felt so emotional.

'But any fool can go into a shop and get an assistant to pick you out the most expensive perfume and jewels. It's the sweet talk that gets a woman into your arms and into your bed!'

'But Andrew, you didn't have to do any of those things to get me into bed.'

'Well, that was because you fancied me something rotten!' He said. Laughing, as he tried to calm down the situation.

184

'I think I'd fallen in love with you a long time ago, but I was with someone else then and you had your lovely Isabel. I wouldn't have broken up your marriage for anything, even though I envied you. But when you and I were both on our own I did think I might stand a chance, and I was right wasn't I?'

'As you always are, my darling girl. Now, to continue, what are we going to do to get Jane and Jake's marriage back on track?'

And that was exactly the question Jessie asked Jane, to which Jane was reluctant to give her an answer.

'The big problem was Jake and I didn't fall in love, we fell in lust! We were like animals in bed. Couldn't get enough of each other's bodies. The only problem was he couldn't tell me he loved me, so I didn't think he did. Does that make sense?'

'Well I understand what you're saying, but are you sure that maybe he couldn't believe his luck to have met and married a wonderful woman like you. Perhaps you intimidated him?'

Jane wanted her say, but Jessie was having none of it.

'You're a very clever woman and he might have problems dealing with clever women? Did you ever tell him you loved him? Did you ever say you couldn't live without him? Did you ever make him feel it was him you wanted to be with, and not just because he'd saved your father's company?'

Jane sat in silence for a few moments, digesting what Jessie had said.

'I don't think Jake knows what love is. He wanted my father's company and thought I should come with the deal! I suppose I was as much to blame, because at first I lusted after his body as well, only my lust quickly changed into love.'

'Why don't you meet him then, before it's too late?' asked Jessie. 'Perhaps he does love you but doesn't know how to tell you?'

Jessie could see Jane was bristling.

'No. I'm sure he doesn't love me. He made it quite clear when we were at the hotel, after I came out of hospital by keeping away; it was as if I disgusted him. And then there was the time when he said he didn't want children, when his mother said she was looking forward to being a grandmother? You were there with me and heard her say that if you remember?'

'But that was because he thought she was interfering. It wasn't her business. It was a matter between the two of you. Whether a couple have children is up to them, not whether a mother-in-law wants grandchildren or not?'

'Well I want children and when I'm divorced, I will find a nice husband, one who wants me for myself. A man who loves me and wants to have children with me!'

It was at this point Jane burst into tears and went into her own office, shutting the door behind her, leaving Jessie shaking her head, knowing there must be some way to end the impasse between her dearest new step daughter, and her new son-in-law, but how? It was quite apparent it was going to take a great deal more than she'd already said to get them back together again. As for Jake, he would have to do his own chasing now. Jessie sighed. There was much more to matchmaking than she had ever thought!

Chapter Twenty

There was a thirteen-year age gap between Jessie and Jane, until now it had never seemed to matter. Somehow though, ever since she'd married Andrew, Jessie had seen a subtle change occur in their relationship and now she felt not only older, but so much wiser in her outlook and especially how she felt about love. It was as though since becoming Jane's stepmother she'd taken on the mantle of responsibility of motherhood and, being with Jane, when she'd been at her most vulnerable, the day she lost her baby, had had a profound effect on Jessie. Her heart had ached, not just for Jane, but for Jake as well. She'd tried hard not to forget his feelings and how he must have felt when his wife lost their baby, a child he'd had no prior knowledge of, until she'd collapsed at his feet! It must have been the shock that had temporarily frozen his feelings. But why didn't Jane tell him she was pregnant as soon as they arrived at the hotel? Was it true only his mother unfortunately speaking out of turn had been the catalyst to the present disaster?

The weeks were passing by, with no hope of getting them together even invitations to spend weekends at the house in the country were refused by both of them, with Jake explaining he had too much work on, as for Jane, her excuses were as many and as varied as his! Excuses such as she had to go somewhere or other with her job, even though Jessie knew other colleagues could easily have done some of her work. It was as though they were both working themselves to the point of exhaustion in their efforts not to see each other.

Then came Christmas and the New Year, both events passing with Jake spending the holidays with his mother and stepfather in Italy, taking Sara back with him as his excuse. She'd completed her first term at college, but was keen to go home. She'd met an attractive young man from Milan who'd been working as a waiter in the hotel during the summer and, as he was going to work at the hotel again over the holidays, it was quite natural she would want to go back home. She'd changed as well since her escapade in London, maturing into a beautiful young woman.

To Jane's surprise, when Sara returned to college in the autumn she'd taken to spending some evenings with her, always talking about Jake. At first it had irked her, but eventually she came to know nearly everything there was to know about the man she'd married in haste, but was now repenting at her leisure!

Andrew and Jessie also began to see another side to Jane. Her mood had finally lightened as her depression lifted and gradually, she was beginning to mellow in her outlook towards Jake. She no longer walked out of the room if Jessie or Andrew spoke of him, which they thought to be a good omen, as they still had visions of them getting back together.

With the Christmas and the New Year festivities over, Jessie knew she was putting on weight. She decided she would have to go to the gym and take some exercise if she was to keep fit and managed to persuade Jane to go with her. Unbeknown to them, Jake had also joined the same gym, aware that eating too much of his mother's wonderful food was beginning to show.

The first evening at the gym, the two girls were given a fitness test where they were weighed, measured and given a small medical examination before they would be allowed anywhere near the equipment. Jane passed without any problem, as her own doctor had already passed her as being fit, when she'd asked his advice about going, mainly if it was safe after her miscarriage? As she only needed to tone her body, she was given the all-clear to go ahead, but not so Jessie.

She was advised to see her own doctor before she was allowed to use any of the equipment. The following day she made an appointment to see him, to get his approval before signing up for the course.

Jessie was stunned after her appointment, so much so she had to sit in the waiting room to recover before going back to her office.

Her doctor had done a complete medical and told her there was no reason why she shouldn't do some light exercise, such as walking and swimming while she was pregnant but definitely nothing too excessive!

'What do you mean, while I'm....' Jessie said, unable to finish her sentence.

The doctor took her hand in his and smiled. 'Exactly what I said Mrs Reynolds, you're pregnant, at least three months, possibly more, but until we do a scan I can't be sure.' Seeing the shocked look on her face he asked her softly. 'Hadn't you realised you were pregnant?'

'No. I hadn't. I thought I was starting to go through the menopause! I'm not a young woman, so it never entered my head I might be pregnant.'

'You're a healthy young woman, newly married, why wouldn't you become pregnant, especially if you don't take any precautions? It's quite a common occurrence, you know?'

He laughed and patted her hand. 'I'll see you next week and we will do that scan, in the meantime, eat well, take plenty of gentle exercise, have lots of fresh air and enjoy being married. You're not ill, you know. You also have a husband who loves you. Make the most of the next few months, because when your baby arrives you will be run off your feet!'

As soon as Jessie walked back into the office, Jane walked across to meet her, to ask how the doctor's appointment had gone, until she saw Jessie's face. She had the look of someone who'd just won millions on the lottery but, before she could speak, Andrew walked into the office.

'Guess what's happened?' Jessie said to him.

Andrew wasn't very good at playing guessing games, especially with Jessie, as he usually lost.

'I don't know what's happened. Instead of me guessing, why don't you just tell me?'

'We're going to have a baby!'

Andrew went pale and, for a moment, he wanted to sit down. Somehow, he managed to keep his composure, which was just as well, as by then Jessie was laughing and crying, at the same time, jumping up and down and twirling Jane, who she'd clasped in her arms in her excitement.

'I can't believe it!' She said. 'All I wanted was to get the "okay" to do some exercises and instead, I find out I'm pregnant. What do you think of that?'

Andrew was by now on his feet with Jessie gathered in his arms, smothering her with kisses; telling her how wonderful she was and was just about to pick up her handbag and take her home when the office door opened and in walked Jake!

Andrew and Jessie stopped kissing. There was a stunned silence for a moment or two, until Jane, wondering what had happened to stop the hilarity, turned and found herself face to face with Jake. She too went pale, as she realised who it was. Suddenly, Jessie reached out to take him by the arm, afraid he would turn tail and run if she wasn't quick enough to stop him. At last, she thought, she had them both in the same place at the same time and now it was up to them! Andrew meanwhile was looking at his wife with a bemused expression on his face as he said.

'Jake, we're going to have a baby!'

Jake wasn't quite sure who Andrew was talking about. Surely, he didn't mean Jane was having a baby. The expression on his face froze, until Jessie took hold of his hand.

'It's me Jake. I'm going to be a mother! What do you think of that?'

'I think that's the most wonderful news I've heard for a long time. I wish you both every happiness, perhaps one day I will be able to tell you the same good news when my wife decides she would like to have my baby?'

All that could be heard in the office was the gasps of shock being exhaled followed by a stunned silence. Andrew and Jessie looked from Jake to Jane. They could see how pale she'd become, and how she was trembling even though she felt rooted to the spot.

Jake walked towards her. 'Sweetheart,' he said. The first time he'd used any term of endearment to her, Jane's eyes widened, her colour quickly changing.

'Darling Jane, I love you. I can't live my life without you. I'm only half a man when you're not with me. I need you. You're my life.'

Everyone in the room could hear the emotion in his voice and his heartfelt plea. Jake was begging. For a while, Jessie and Andrew clutched at each other, willing Jane to have pity on him.

As for Jane, her legs were threatening to buckle under her at any moment and she knew she must sit down before she fell in a heap on the floor, but there was no fear of her falling as Jake had taken hold of her, steadying her, oblivious of Jessie, Andrew.

All she saw was Jake was crushing Jane to his chest, his lips searching for hers, and then kissing her with such intensity, it was as though his very life depended on her lips.

Jane couldn't believe what was happening either: her amber-eyed pirate had come for her, he'd finally rescued her and, at that moment she knew, without a shadow of doubt that they would be together, for always.

Nothing would ever part them again!

Epilogue

With the divorce papers cancelled, and as soon as could be arranged, Jane and Jake had their marriage blessed in the old church in the village. All their friends and families were gathered around them on a glorious day that was full of promise for their future. As they renewed their wedding vows before the altar, Jake placed her wedding ring back on the finger where it so rightly belonged and, for the second time, he gallantly kissed her hand. At that moment, Jane knew her father had been right, some arranged marriages can be successful and she intended hers to be the proof that he was right. As for Jake, he knew by finally opening his heart he'd at last found a pirate treasure that could never be surpassed. He held the biggest prize of all in his arms as he kissed his wife, vowing he would love this wonderful woman for the rest of his life, and beyond. And then, when they were alone, he promised himself he would put all his loving thoughts into actions. This time, Jane would be in no doubt he loved her, not just for now, but forever and beyond.

For the first time, the fates finally agreed between themselves that now Jane and Jake were together once more and truly in love, their work was done.

All I can say is long may love live!

THE END